THE
GENTLEMAN
IN ROOM 205

Tambra,
  Thanks so much for
your support!

Much Love

Bart Harper

BART HARPER

WASTELAND PRESS
Shelbyville, KY USA
www.wastelandpress.net

The Gentleman in Room 205
by Bart Harper

First Printing—June 2009
ISBN: 978-1-60047-317-3

Printed in the U.S.A.

Acknowledgments

This book could not have been possible without the following people.

Thank you to:
My wife and kids for their love and support.
My mother for always being there.
My father for inspiring me to write this book.
My editors, Jamey Booterbaugh and Vickie Shultz.
My illustrator, Lewis A. White Jr.
My friends for proofreading and feedback.
My publisher, Tim, for his hard work and imagination.
Lisa Wolfe, Ann Carper, Rachel Long, and Tara Parsons
for marketing

A special thank you to:
Uncle Sonny, Uncle Ralph, Aunt Norma, and Aunt Georgia
for being there every day with my father. You truly were a
blessing to us all!

Be sure to check out Author Bart Harper on Facebook,
Twitter, and Myspace for special discounts and stories.

Also available:

Adventures of a Fat Kid by Bart Harper.

Prologue

"Unleash it," he would yell as I sprinted full speed towards him. I would wrap my arms around his legs and try to bring him down, but he was iron, indestructible. "Iron man" they called him back in his college days, and I had a lot to live up to. Springtime was the same every year. The first sunny day would prove to be a torturous five hours of passing, catching, and, of course, tackling.

Football was life, at least to him. I would have rather curled up with a good book or played a game of chess, but I would never have let him know. He was a great father. He always put me first. I admired him and felt like I owed it to him to try to love the sport that had made him a legend.

I had the talent and the ability, even at the early age of 10. When I hit him, he would smile at the crashing sound. He would send me out to catch over 200 passes each day, and often, he aimed the pass high so that I would have to leap to pull it in. Then came the handoffs, over a hundred each day, and with each one, I would have to sprint 50 yards to the end zone. It was an intense workout.

Because my father had been a football hero in our community, people would often stop by and watch the backyard practices. There were always comments about Dad's old ballgames and his amazing abilities on the football field. His fans would inquire about the time he knocked another player unconscious with a vicious tackle or another time when he scored six touchdowns against the top-ranked team in the state. Dad was always glad to tell the stories over and over.

The visitors would often witness my sprints or a leaping catch and tell my father that I was chip off of the old block. Dad would smile proudly.

It was hard to do something that I didn't enjoy. As I look back though, those were some of the best days that I have ever experienced. It's funny how time changes your outlook on certain events.

I played football for four years, and I still remember the day that I told him. At the end of my eighth-grade season, I had made the decision.

We went out for pizza to celebrate our championship, just the two of us. I guess he noticed that I was depressed because he initiated the conversation by asking me what was wrong. There was no concealing it, so I bluntly told him that I didn't want to play football anymore.

I remember the disappointment on his face and wishing that I could take back the words. He asked me why, so I told him the truth. It was not in my heart and he had to know it. He never said so, but that day was difficult for him. It was as if his football career had ended all over again.

Then, he did something that I will never forget. He stood up right there in that restaurant and walked around the table to where I was sitting. He told me to stand in his usual militant voice. I did as he ordered; not knowing what was coming next. He put his hands on my shoulders and looked deeply into my eyes. I looked away in shame, avoiding the eye contact. I knew that I had hurt him and that was the last thing that I wanted to do.

"Look at me, young man!" he said intently.

I stared back at him as he told me that he had never seen such talent on the football field. Those words still ring in my ear from time to time as a reminder of what I threw away.

"You are the best that I've ever seen! But you should have told me this a long time ago! You should never do something if your heart is not in it. Yes, you have all the talent in the world, but without heart, you will never be great," he said.

I knew he was right; I hung my head. My heart was breaking for him. I knew how much he wanted it, and I was afraid that he wouldn't love me or want to spend time with me without football. He must have read my mind because he pulled me closer and put his arms around me.

"I love football. I love it- the sound of helmets clashing or the feeling of scoring a last-minute touchdown. But I love you more than anything. I want you to be happy, and that is all that matters to me," he whispered.

He hadn't uttered those words often, but that heartfelt statement changed me. It changed our relationship. I thought that he only loved me for football, and that is why I had been so fearful of quitting. At that moment, I realized that it didn't matter what I did from that point on. My father would always love me. It was a special bond between us that could never be broken.

I squeezed him hard and whispered back, "I love you too, Dad. I love you too!"

Chapter One

I walked past him every day on my way to visit my father. He was a tall man with massive hands, and I remember thinking that he must have been quite strapping in his day. It seemed that every time I saw Mr. Rent, he always had a smile on his face. Even though I didn't know him, I couldn't help but like him.

I had always been a shy person. I guess you could say that I had a wall up. Some people took it the wrong way. They would call me cocky or stuck up, but with Mr. Rent it was different. I found myself wanting to talk to him for some odd reason. His welcoming attitude and friendly manner were very inviting. I didn't have many friends, and I was going through a very difficult time in my life. I really needed someone to talk to, but I had no idea who would want to listen to my problems. I was alone in the world, and I was losing my only friend.

My father was my hero, but even heroes die. He was just one of those special people who gave all he had to everyone else. He had grown up as poor as a church mouse. Raised in a family of fifteen kids, he had struggled all of his life to better his situation. He was a determined man who would not let poverty get him down.

His first claim to fame had been on the football field. The year was 1966, and he was just seventeen years old. With unbelievable speed, he shattered high school rushing records across our home state. He had made his family so proud, and it was just the beginning.

In his hometown of Rolling Hills, he achieved great success becoming a teacher, a father, and a businessman in the community that had looked down on his family for so long. Through hard work and determination, he brought a new-found respect to his family name.

I guess it was because he grew up so poor, but my father was the most unselfish person I knew. When it came to me, he always put my needs before his own. I think he just didn't want me to have to do without the way that he had all of those years. He treated me like every kid wants to be treated. I was his best friend, too.

Now my father just laid there in his bed. The once proud young man had grown old and weak. He could make eye contact, but he could not speak. It had been a difficult battle but with every day, he was losing. The stroke had been a deadly one affecting his motion and speech. My father was living a nightmare from which he could not awaken.

With so many medical needs, I was forced to put him in the home. I had found him a private room so that I could decorate it just like his old house. He had a recliner, a television, and anything else I could find to make him feel at home. Luckily, I found a nursing facility close to where I lived. I visited him three times a day to make sure the nurses were doing their jobs. I knew that he was frightened, and I had to be there for him as often as possible.

Thank goodness for Lena! She was Dad's favorite nurse. His eyes would shine when she entered the room. Now, my father had always been a lady's man, so the fact that Lena was young, blonde, and beautiful didn't hurt. I sat there with him for several weeks, and he hadn't responded to me that much. But when Lena asked him to give her a "thumbs up," he suddenly became Mr. Cool, and made a very willing attempt. I always felt at ease when Lena was on duty.

She was a big hit with all of the patients, so I thought she probably knew some things about Mr. Rent. Where was he from? Was he married or did he have a family? For some reason, I was curious about the gentleman in room 205.

I walked into the nursing home late one night to check on Dad. As I strolled by Mr. Rent's room, I noticed that he was not sitting in his chair as usual. I peeked in to see if he was sleeping. I had a bad feeling, for it was common to go visit a loved one on Friday, and on Saturday they were gone, dead. Life is fragile at the Niletree Nursing Home.

I snuck into the room, careful not to wake him, but Mr. Rent was nowhere to be found. I noticed some candy wrappers that had fallen on the floor and a pair of brown slippers beside the bed. Then, I heard him.

"Please, help me!" he cried.

He was curled up in the corner. He had obviously fallen out of bed, so I ran to him to help him up.

He smiled and said, "I'm glad you came along, young man."

I told him that it was no problem as I helped him back into his bed. I thought it to be strange that he was so weak because he had always seemed so sturdy. Most of the patients walked with a cane or used a wheelchair, but not Mr. Rent. He seemed healthy and his mind was sharp and coherent. I often wondered why he was even in the home.

Mr. Rent flicked the lights on and stated, "I've seen you here almost every day, young man. Is that your father in 208?"

As I told him my story, he listened intently. It felt good to discuss my dad, my life, and the tragic stroke. We had only just met, but he seemed like an old friend. We chatted for about an hour before I realized that it was getting late. I told him that I appreciated the conversation, but that I had to go visit my father.

He smiled and said, "Come back tomorrow, young man."

I nodded and told him that I would, and asked him if there was anything that I could bring him.

He said, "I would kill for a bag of peppermints. I'm not supposed to have them, but they have been my favorite ever since I was a boy."

I told the old man that I would go to the store and pick up the goodies. He smiled, yawned, and closed his eyes. As I stepped out of the room, I turned off the light. I usually felt sad when I was at the home, but just for a second, my heart was at peace.

When I entered my dad's room, Lena was giving him a breathing treatment. I asked him if he had given her a kiss yet, and he responded with a devious grin.

Lena laughed and said, "He has only tried once tonight!"

I told Dad that he might be losing his touch, but he very faintly shook his head in denial. As Lena left the room, I sat on the edge of the bed. I ran my fingers through his hair as he stared up at me. His beautiful blue eyes told the sad story. I knew that he wanted to say something. His eyes would get big, and he would try to make motions with his hand. The stroke had taken almost everything, but it never took his heart. I like to think that he simply wanted to say "I love you." We sat there in complete silence, and I said a special prayer. The prayer was always the same. I would hold his hand and say, "Please Lord, reach down and give him strength. Put the life back into his limbs. Show us the way Lord. Show us the way."

As I continued to pray, Dad fell asleep. I held his hand tighter and cried because I knew that the road ahead was going to be hard. I knew that my father's condition was getting worse and that it was just a matter of time. My worst fear was becoming a reality. I was losing my best friend, and there was nothing I could do about it.

It seemed so unfair for someone like him to have to endure such suffering. He had helped so many people over the years. He had always remembered where he came from, and as a teacher he gave so much of himself. He had often bought shoes for those students who were less fortunate, and it was a common practice to give his last ten dollars to someone who really needed it.

He was a good person, and he protected those that he loved. I flashed back to the time when I was nine years old and Dad was driving us home from the movies. My sister and I were in the back and Mom was in the passenger seat. All of a sudden, the car behind us started flashing its lights and swerving across the center line. Dad quickly pulled the car over to let the driver by, but the car followed us off the road. Two guys got out and walked towards our car. They were obviously drunk out of their minds, cussing and stumbling. Dad got out and met them halfway. They had endangered his family, and he was not happy. The men continued to swear, and one of them swung at my father. My sister and I watched the whole thing out the back window. Our eyes widened as Dad grabbed one of the guys by the throat and lifted him off the ground. The other drunk came up behind him and struck Dad in the back of the head. Dad turned and threw the one man back about ten yards. He backhanded the other maniac in the nose. As the blood gushed, both men laid on the ground half unconscious. He got back into the car, and my sister and I cheered with glee. I informed Dad that he reminded me of The Masked Muscle, my favorite wrestler, and he laughed. Like I said earlier, he was my hero.

As I relived that episode, I couldn't believe that someone as strong and dynamic as my father could deteriorate so quickly. It seemed that ever since he fell ill, I would think back to those days when I was a little boy.

Whether it was those days of throwing the football in the backyard or fishing in the creek, the memories helped me get through the day. Sometimes, memories are all we have!

I sat down in the chair and turned on the television. I flipped through the channels until I found his favorite show. While Little Joe and Hoss beat up the bad guys, I noticed something glistening on the night stand. I got up and walked across the room to inspect the mysterious objects. I stood there confused as I counted two candy wrappers. I picked them up and lifted them to my nose. Just as I suspected, they smelled of peppermint.

Chapter Two

I received the call at three in the morning. It was the hospital again. I was getting accustomed to the early morning calls. Dad had coughing spells that would interfere with his breathing. The doctor said that it was pneumonia, and it was caused by his immobility.

He said, "The more he lies around, the more chance of pneumonia and infection!"

Every few days, I would get the call that he was having trouble breathing, and I would rush to the hospital. I would run to his side to let him know that I was there. I knew my father, and I knew that he wanted me with him just in case something bad happened. On several occasions, the doctor would tell me to let him go, but I would ask my father. People often didn't realize that he was coherent. Just because his face was paralyzed, didn't mean that he didn't know what was going on. I would ask him if he wanted the ventilator, and he would respond with a slight head nod. The doctors would always act surprised to see that he understood. Dad was ventilated over five times. I can't imagine how scary that would be.

I dropped the phone and put on my shoes. I drove as fast as I could to get to him. The nurses had medicated him, and he had calmed down. The coughing had ceased, and he seemed to be asleep. As I walked up to him, his eyes opened. I put my arms around him and put my head on his chest. I thought back to those days when I was just a little boy. Many nights I had slept with my head on my dad's chest. He would rub my head just like I did for him now. It always made me feel safe. I guess some things never change.

Suddenly, I felt something in my hair. I gasped and sat up. It was my dad's fingers. He hadn't been able to pick up his hand in months, yet his hand moved from the back of my head to my face.

I laughed and said, "Dad, you old scallywag!"

He let out a moan and smiled back. For the first time in months, I saw a glimmer of hope. If his hand could heal, then his leg could heal. Maybe he could get better. Maybe he could survive this. Those thoughts ran through my head for the rest of the morning.

They took him back to the nursing home that day. Lena was waiting in the doorway as the ambulance pulled up. She escorted the medics to his room, and she personally tucked him into bed. Dad looked very content. I think he was just happy about his new improvement and the fact that Lena had to bend over to pick up his blanket. As she knelt, his hand wandered.

"Oh, what the heck?" she squealed.

She turned around to look at my father who was grinning like he had just shot the sheriff.

She giggled and said, "Mr. Harper! How did you do that?"

We all laughed and rejoiced about Dad's new ability. Lena had just been violated, and she couldn't have been happier. As I told her about Dad's arm and hand, other nurses came in to see if it was true. They all gave him a big hug, and of course, he made many other grabbing attempts. His life had been so terrible for so long, but on that night, he finally got to experience a little happiness.

When everyone had left the room, I grabbed his hand and said our prayer. As I said the words, Dad reached up and rested his hand on my shoulder. I was so happy that I could barely contain myself.

I whispered to him, "You can do it, Pop! Never give up!"

Just sitting in that room was difficult. I would talk to him often and pretend like nothing was wrong. Most of the time, I would sit and watch television with him or read him the paper. Sometimes I would think about all the things that we had gone through over the years. Dad was no stranger to the concept of determination. He had made it through so many horrible things in his lifetime. Ten years ago, he had fought a battle with the devil and in good ole Dad fashion, he had come out victorious. He was only forty-eight at the time, and he had suffered a severe stroke. He laid in a coma for weeks, and the whole right side of his body had been paralyzed. I was with him every day in the hospital. I held his head as he vomited and did physical therapy on his legs and arms. I had refused to let him die, and one day he simply woke up. He could talk, but he was very weak. Little by little, we beat the devil, the demon illness that was trying to take him. The doctors said that Dad should have died there in that hospital, but instead he had survived. My father was a survivor, no doubt about it.

I was no stranger to this situation either. Dad was ten years older now, and the new stroke had taken his other side. His entire body was paralyzed, the devil was back to take him. But with his hand and arm coming back, we both knew that there was a chance. I drifted off in the chair with a smirk on my face and a renewed faith in my heart.

The next day, Lena awakened me with a little nudge. She had a cup of coffee and a donut.

"Figured you might be hungry after all the excitement," she said.

I told her thank you and took the goodies. I was famished. As I took a bite, I couldn't help but notice the tube that was sticking out of my Dad's stomach. It led to a bottle of brown fluid. Every few seconds the timer would go off, and the fluid would flow into his body. My appetite faded. It was hard to eat in front of him. He had lived for food. It was his favorite thing to do. We would go out to eat at least three times a week together. Dad was a short, chubby guy who loved life and food. His 265-pound frame had dwindled to a sickly 160 pounds. I put the donut down and went for a walk to get some air.

As I opened the door to go out of the building, I heard someone yell, "Young man! Where have you been?"

It was Mr. Rent. He limped towards me with a friendly smile. I told him about my father and his breathing problems, and we sat down in the lobby and talked for little while.

"So where is that candy? I'm going through sugar withdrawal" he joked.

"Oh, I'm sorry, Sir. I forgot about it, but I'll pick you some up tonight," I replied.

He laughed and asked me about my father. He went on to tell me a little about his adoptive father who had passed away when he was just a boy.

"It's never easy to lose someone you love," he stated.

We talked about all of the things that my father had overcome, and surprisingly he could relate. He told me that he had been adopted at an early age, and that he hadn't known his real parents. They had been killed in some sort of accident when he was just a baby. He was careful with the details which made me more curious. His life had not been easy, and that made him and my father two of a kind.

With his real family gone and his adoptive father dead, he had been raised by his adoptive mother in a small town in the mid-west. He had gone to work at the age of ten to help support his mother and their struggling farm.

"There were times when food was scarce," he added.

As I sat and listened, I thought about the stories my father had told me about his family and the hard times. I remembered that he had totally grossed me out when he mentioned a groundhog stew that Grandma would prepare for all the kids. It had always made me feel so proud of my father to know where he came from and the things that he had endured. I guess some people would have been ashamed, but I knew that Dad's life experiences had made him the wonderful person he had become.

At one point during our conversation, I started to ask Mr. Rent if he had been in my father's room. The candy wrappers that I had found on my father's nightstand were the same as the ones I had noticed in his room. I chickened out, though. If he wanted me to know that he had been in there, then he would have told me. It really didn't matter to me either way, but any extra attention for Dad was appreciated. I couldn't be there twenty-four seven, and he had some very special needs.

I finally stood up and said, "Well, I think I'm going to go to town and pick up that candy. I wouldn't want you to go into sugar shock!"

He laughed and commented, "Perhaps we can do some trading."

I just winked and walked out the door. I had no idea what he meant, but I wanted nothing in return. He was an old man, and he couldn't have anything that I needed. I just wanted to do a good deed for someone who was alone like me. Little did I know that Mr. Rent had much more to give than I could ever imagine.

Chapter Three

The next day I got up early and went to visit my father and my new friend. I was always relieved in the morning because it meant that Dad had made it for another day. I put the two bags of peppermints in my coat pocket, and I was off. I found myself looking forward to seeing Mr. Rent. He had a way of explaining things and making me feel better about my whole situation. I had been so wrapped up in the terrible things that were happening to me that I had forgotten that other people were going through the same types of situations. Mr. Rent had taken me in from the storm, and it made me realize that perhaps I could do the same for some of the other patients.

I stopped by the store and bought ten more bags of candy. I figured I would sneak some to the other patients and perhaps make some new friends. I chuckled to myself as I entered the nursing home. I felt like Santa Claus, and the residents were my kids awaiting their gifts. Of course, I had to stop at Mr. Rent's first. He had been so excited when I had mentioned that I would get him the candy. I couldn't wait to see his face and chat awhile.

As I strolled up to his door, I noticed it was ajar. I peeked around, and there was nobody there. I figured that he was probably in the cafeteria, so I decided to put the candy on his bed. I reached into my pocket and pulled out the two bags. As I put them on his pillow, I noticed a cardboard box beside the sink. It was loaded full with what looked like newspaper articles. I looked around to make sure that nobody was watching, and I walked closer to inspect the contents. I picked up a few of the headlines. Then, I reached into the box and pulled out a few more. The newspapers were from all around the world, and they all had common themes. The headlines were mostly disasters that had occurred over the last fifty years. Earthquakes, terrorist attacks, and floods were just a few of the topics. I thought it to be very odd that someone would want to collect old headlines of this sort. Maybe I didn't know Mr. Rent as well as I thought. What kind of person would get enjoyment out of other people's misery? I left the room with a heavy heart and a doubtful mind.

I walked down the hall towards my father's room. Lena passed by and I asked, "How is he today?"

She smiled and said, "Didn't anyone tell you?" She took my hand and hurried me to his room.

As I walked in, Dad turned his head to look at me. He slowly raised his hand and waved. Then, he raised his other hand and gave me the patented "thumbs up." I nearly fainted. A tear ran down my face as I kissed him. How was this happening? It was a true miracle. My father had regained the use of his right and left arm in a matter of days. My heart pounded with joy as I took Lena's left hand and Dad took her right. We said our usual prayer which was obviously working. The Lord was answering our plea one day at a time.

When the doctor made his rounds that day, he got a big surprise when he visited room 208. We had Dad sitting up in a chair ready for action.

Dr. Enal had been our family physician for many years, and he and Dad had been good friends. Every day when he came in to check on Dad, he would say "Dan, give me some skin today!" He was always trying to motivate him to make the attempt, but every day Doc would have to settle for a very faint eye blink. That day would prove to be different.

Doc entered and said, "Big Dan! What are you doing in that chair?"

Dad smirked and held out his hand as if to say, "Give me five, Doc!"

Dr. Enal looked at me in amazement and asked me when it had happened.

Lena interrupted, "Just this morning, Doctor! It happened overnight."

Doc turned to Dad and gave him the high five and a big hug.

Dr. Enal laughed and said, "Your Dad never ceases to amaze me!"

"Yeah, Doc. Me too!" I replied proudly.

A little later that day, I went to look for Mr. Rent to tell him the great news. He was sitting in his chair reading.

I said, "Hello Sir! Did you get your candy?"

"Yes, young man, thank you!" he cheerfully replied.

I told him about Dad, and he laughed, "You just can't keep a good man down, can you?"

His face wrinkled as he smiled. I suddenly forgot about the newspaper headlines that I had seen earlier. This man seemed so kind. Surely, there had to be some logical explanation as to why he owned such things. Perhaps one day he would tell me.

In all the excitement, I had forgotten to make my rounds to pass out the candy to the other patients. The next day when I visited, I took my basket full of peppermints and other goodies and went from room to room. It felt good to do something nice for someone, and it gave me a chance to meet some very special people. I also figured that some of the other residents may have known some information about Mr. Rent. I was still very curious about him. It wasn't my intent to spy on him, but I had an inquiring mind and just had to know more.

I had stopped at every room, except one. The name on the door said "Mrs. Ressler." I knocked and waited.

When she answered the door, I said, "Hello, Mrs. Ressler!"

She stared at me for a second and replied, "You must have the wrong room! My name is Jane Kessler."

I apologized and pointed out the name on her door. She laughed and stated, "Oh! Those aides can't spell for nothing!"

She told me to come in and have a seat, so I entered and sat down on the side of her bed. As I asked her if she would like a bag of candy, she picked up a marker and went to change her name on the white board.

"These darn dry erase markers! All those other patients roam the halls and rub against my door. They erase my name all the time! Those aides can't spell anything. I have to do it myself!" she explained.

I giggled a little at her lively remarks. She was spunky for eighty years old. She accepted the candy and exclaimed, "Peppermint has always been my favorite!"

I figured that peppermint must have been pretty popular back in the early 1900's since almost every patient had made that statement.

We sat and chatted for a few minutes before I brought up the topic of Mr. Rent. None of the other residents had known much about him besides the fact that he was a loner. Mrs. Kessler was my last chance. She smiled when I mentioned the gentleman in room 205.

"Oh yes! I don't know him well, but he seems like a nice man," she said.

I asked how long he had been at the home and she stated that it had been several months.

"I'm not really sure why he came here! He has always been healthy and very able. That is, until the last few days," she said sadly.

We went on to talk about Mr. Rent's new health problems. He had fallen out of bed, and he now walked with a slight limp. She stated that it was odd for him to show weakness.

I added, "Yes, he has always seemed very sturdy for his age."

I told Mrs. Kessler about my father and his vast improvements over the last few days.

She smiled and said, "Maybe it's that candy he has been eating."

My face tuned white, and I asked how she knew about the candy. She went on to tell me that she had seen the old gentleman enter my father's room. She had snuck down late one night to see just what he was doing. Patients were not allowed to be in there, and she told me that she was going to tell the head nurse.

"He was holding a beautiful crystal," she stated.

I was at a loss for words and thought perhaps she was confused. She was an old woman and at that age things get jumbled. She went on to say that as the old gent had held the crystal over my father's head, he had taken a piece of peppermint from his pocket. He had opened the candy and fed my father a piece.

"My dad can't eat! His mouth is paralyzed!" I added.

She apologized for upsetting me and said, "Maybe I should have just kept that to myself!"

I told her that it was okay and that I would handle it. As I left her room, she thanked me for the candy. I closed the door and thought to myself once again that she was an old lady. She had probably dreamed that whole thing. Then I remembered the wrappers that I had found. It couldn't have been true.

Chapter Four

"Stop! Slow down! Don't run in the hallway!" the orderly shouted.

The little boy didn't pay attention. He zoomed by the rooms and did a baseball slide as he reached the exit door. As he let out a joyful howl, all the patients peeked out of their rooms to witness the disturbance. We all laughed as Max rose to his feet and smiled at us. He was so young, so energetic, and I am sure he brought back memories to all the elderly patients who now could barely walk let alone run. Even I was a bit envious to see such joy and innocence in the little boy's face. I remembered those carefree days and longed to go back, just for a day.

Our pleasure was interrupted by Lena shrieking, "How many times have I told you not to run in the hallway, Max? Get over here now!"

The little boy smirked as she took him by his arm and led him to a time-out chair. He winked at Mrs. Kessler who was still chuckling as he received his scolding. Max was Lena's only son, and that was probably a good thing since he was quite a handful. But she loved him, and he loved her.

"Just a growing boy," Mrs. Kessler would say to defend her young friend.

She and Max had struck up a friendship from the very first time she met him. She had been cleaning her room one day, and Max had snuck away from his mother again. He had crept into the old lady's room to hide under her bed. He loved to play hide and seek but had not mastered the whole idea of the game. When Mrs. Kessler decided to clean under her bed, she got a big surprise, as did the boy. With her handy broom, she reached under the bed to sweep and then heard a loud cry. She had hit Max in the eye with some of the old-fashioned straw and nearly blinded the rascal. He came out from under the bed and nearly gave Mrs. Kessler a heart attack. He wailed and moaned until the old lady handed him a homemade cookie and her carton of milk. After that, they became the best of friends, and when Max would visit, he would often spend time with the friendly old lady.

Max visited the nursing home at least once a week, and he had made many friends among the other patients. In fact, everyone loved Max. That is, everyone but Mr. Pyle. Of course, Mr. Pyle didn't like anyone. He sat in the corner of his room and stared out the window. If you heard him speak, it would almost always be something negative. Most of the time, he just yelled at the doctors, nurses, aides, and of course, Max.

Even though Lena had told him numerous times to stay out of Mr. Pyle's room, he just didn't understand the concept of irritable people. Max was one of those kids who loved everyone and would be nice to everyone, even old, grumpy people and even Mr. Pyle. With his light blonde hair and soft, green eyes, he could eventually win over even the most agitated heart, but not Robert Pyle.

Life had been hard for the old man, hard enough to make his face turn to stone and his humanity wilt. Lena had told me his history one day over coffee, and I remember becoming more tolerable of the old fellow. He had fought in World War II along with his younger brother Frank. He had practically raised Frank since their father had passed away early in the boy's lives. They had enlisted together and had requested that they serve in the same unit. As the older brother, he was always looking out for Frank, but during the total chaos of battle, confusion happens.

They had been under fire for three days, and the two brothers lay side by side in a shallow bunker. Ammunition was growing short. Greatly outnumbered, there were only a dozen soldiers left and they were trapped. Someone had to make a move and they knew what had to be done.

A lonely tank with a heavy gun sat only fifty yards away. Someone would have to sprint to the tank and provide cover while the other soldiers escaped, and it had to be done soon. Robert Pyle was now in charge and announced that he was going to make a run for it, even though he knew it meant certain death. He ordered the soldiers to provide the cover, but as he said the words, his brother took off towards the tank. Frank was already 25 yards across the field when the bullet hit him in the chest and then another in the left arm. Robert Pyle ran towards his dying brother, but it was too late. Shouting and shooting, Robert jumped on top of his brother who was now gasping for air. He dragged Frank to safety and placed him behind the tank. He jumped up on the metal beast and began firing the heavy gun like a man possessed, and the soldiers retreated. Mr. Pyle evidently saved the lives of every man who was trapped in that bunker. He saved everyone except his little brother who died right there on that battlefield.

After the war, he was never the same. He had married but lost his wife to cancer several years back. He had one son who had passed away at the age of nine. Yes, Mr. Pyle had lived a hard life. Everything he had ever loved had gone away. Now he had given up and was simply waiting to die. I felt sorry for the old man and in many ways, I could understand his misery.

Chapter Five

Over the next week, Dad seemed to get stronger and stronger. He was now able to hold the television remote and the dumbbell weights that I had bought him for his birthday. His neck muscles were getting stronger, and he could answer yes or no questions by nodding his head. Before, the nods had been so faint that you could barely tell what he was trying to say, but now his ability left no doubt. It was like a dream come true, and we were winning the battle once again.

I hadn't visited Mr. Rent much because I was afraid of what I would say. The whole crystal and candy incident was on my mind often. I really wanted to know more, but my shy persona kept me quiet. If I wanted answers, I would have to find out for myself.

I waited until I saw Mr. Rent go to lunch. He limped by Mr. Pyle's room, and I was shocked at how poorly he looked. His face was pale. He was hunched over a bit more than usual. I walked into his room to do a little investigating. I felt like Sherlock Holmes trying to solve a mystery. Of course, Mr. Rent had not committed any crime that I knew of. He was only guilty of being a good friend. I felt tense as I looked through his closet, but I had to find it. If I found the crystal, it would confirm her story. Only then would I confront Mr. Rent.

I searched the room for ten minutes, but found nothing besides the old box of newspapers. I let out a sigh of relief. I didn't want to find anything that would contaminate the newfound friendship. As I turned to exit the room, there stood Mr. Rent with a puzzled look on his face.

"What are you doing, young man? Is there something you need?" he muttered.

I smiled a nervous smile and stated, "Oh, I was just looking for you, Sir! I thought maybe you were out of peppermints."

He slowly walked over to the closet, and I took a deep breath. I hoped that he wouldn't notice that I had searched through it.

He opened the closet door and said, "Now where did I put that blanket?"

He pulled out an old, red blanket and added, "This is for your dad."

As he handed it to me, I told him that he didn't have to give me anything.

He said, "I told you we were gonna do some trading, now didn't I?"

I unfolded the blanket and examined the texture. It was a thin material, hardly appropriate for cold nights, and the color had faded a bit. Not wanting to hurt the old man's feelings, I told him that it was a beautiful quilt and that my father would love it.

The old man went on to tell me that the blanket had belonged to his real father and that it was very special to him.

"Oh, Sir! I can't accept it! It should stay in your family!" I exclaimed.

He said, "Now, young man, you are going to take it! It is a gift for you and your father."

He told me that he had no family to leave it to and that he would appreciate it if I took care of it for him. Of course, I couldn't say no. I considered it an honor.

"Your dad needs it more than I do now!" he continued.

I knew the old blanket wouldn't be able to keep Dad warm, but I figured I could fold it up and store it safely in his closet.

I put my hand on Mr. Rent's shoulder and responded with a sincere, "Thank you, Sir, I'll treasure it."

He smiled and said, "I know you will, young man."

The next day I packed some things in my duffle. I would be spending the night with my father, and would be playing detective once again. My plan was simple. I wanted to catch Mr. Rent in the act. I wanted to see just how my father could have eaten that peppermint.

It was around ten o'clock, and Dad was already asleep. I walked by Mr. Rent's room and told him goodnight just to make him think that I was leaving as usual. Then, I turned and went to my dad's room and placed the recliner behind the door. I placed two huge quilts on the chair that would serve as my camouflage just in case the midnight visitor showed. I took my evening vitamins, drank a glass of tea, and drifted off.

It was two in the morning when I awoke. I rubbed my eyes and proceeded to the restroom. I put my hand on the doorknob to reenter the room when I heard a squeak. I cracked the door to see out into the darkness. To my surprise, it was Mr. Rent. My heart started beating faster and my legs began to shake nervously. It was so dark I could barely make out what he was holding in his hand. Then, there was aglow. The object lit up to expose the crystal. He stood over my father who was now wide awake.

"Hello, Danny!" he said.

The old man took the glimmering crystal and placed it above Dad's head.

"This crystal belonged to my father and to his father before him!" he chanted.

He touched my dad's forehead with the crystal, and the light dimmed. Dad reached up and took the old man's hand. He opened his mouth, and Mr. Rent smiled.

"I know, Danny! I know!" he giggled.

He pulled out a single piece of peppermint and took off the wrapper. As I watched my father chew the candy, I sobbed quietly. It was such a precious moment that I could not disturb them. I didn't know what kind of magic this was, but I knew it couldn't be bad. All I knew was that my father was getting healthy and that was the only thing that mattered. I would leave Mr. Rent to it, fearful that he would stop the healing.

I waited in the bathroom until the old man had left and Dad was asleep. I kissed him on the cheek and sat down in the recliner. My mind raced as I relived what had just happened. Mr. Rent was obviously some sort of witch doctor or something. I was thankful to him, but I was also scared to death.

In the morning, I peeked into Mr. Rent's room to see if he was still sleeping. He was awake, but he didn't look well. I went to his side and asked him if he was alright. He could not answer me. I called for the nurse. Lena came in and checked his pulse. She quickly called the hospital to arrange for an ambulance. I stayed by his side until they came. As they took him away, I told him that everything was going to be okay and that I would come see him in a little while. He took my hand and firmly squeezed it.

I went back to my father's room to get my keys out of my jacket. When I entered the room, Dad was sitting in the chair. Lena came in to check on him as well.

"Well, Mr. Harper. Looks like you are going to watch some television today!" she joked.

I looked at her and asked, "Didn't you put him in the chair?"

She gave me a confused look and said, "I thought you did."

We both turned to stare at Dad who was holding the remote. He smiled and gave us a big "thumbs up!"

Chapter Six

At the hospital, Mr. Rent was not doing very well. He was so weak that he couldn't stand and his speech was slurred and limited. I asked the nurse if they knew what was wrong with my friend, but they were at a loss. The doctors were not sure why the old man had gone downhill so quickly. Only weeks before, he had been the healthiest patient at Niletree, and now he could barely function.

I stood over him while he slept and said a prayer. "I don't know who or what you are, Sir, but you are a good man. That is easy to see. Please, God help him." I whispered.

His eyes opened and we stared silently at one another. He tried to say something, but the words were difficult. I leaned down closer, and he whispered back to me, "the red blanket!"

I asked him if he wanted it, and he shook his head.

"For your father," he continued.

I told him that Dad had the blanket, and that everything was fine. I informed him about the mass improvements that he had made and that we were sure he had stood by himself. In his weakened state, I found myself wanting to tell him about the crystal. I wanted to let him know that I saw and was thankful, but I was afraid to upset him. Just as I got up enough courage, he closed his eyes and was asleep.

"Another time, Sir," I concluded.

Back at Niletree, Dad kept improving. As I entered the front doors, two of the nurses ran to me.

"You gotta see this," the young man stated.

We hurried to his room, and there he stood.

"He has been standing for ten minutes all by himself," Lena exclaimed.

I couldn't believe my own eyes. I went to him and told him how proud I was of him.

"We never gave up, did we, Pop?" I cried.

He opened his mouth like he wanted to say something but all he could muster was a low moan. I put my arms around him and said, "Patience, Dad. That will be the next thing we work on! Before you know it, you will be eating a steak."

He smiled and everyone laughed. In that moment of unbelievable joy, I couldn't help but think of Mr. Rent. I just knew that he had given me back my best friend. Perhaps he was an angel sent down to help me. I had prayed so many times that maybe God had listened. Whatever the case, my father was a living miracle and everyone knew it.

Over the next few days, I worked with my father on standing and sitting. I massaged his face trying to stimulate those muscles. He was opening his mouth and breathing much better. I asked the doctor about letting him eat something, but Doc said, "I'm afraid you father still cannot swallow well."

I thought about the candy that Mr. Rent had given Dad, but I didn't dare say anything. I figured that the crystal had something to do with the fact that he was able to swallow it. I would have to ask Mr. Rent about it soon. I could tell that Dad was hungry because every time I mentioned anything edible, his eyes would almost pop out of his head. It must be a terrible thing not to be able to eat.

I visited Mr. Rent when I could, but most of my attention went to my father. The old man had been in the hospital for a week when it started. I went to visit Mr. Rent and noticed a vast improvement. He was sitting up eating a bowl of hospital soup when I opened the door.

"Hello, young man," he uttered. His color was much better, and he seemed much stronger than the last time I had seen him.

"Looks like you are doing well, Sir," I stated.

He told me that he was feeling better and that he should be coming back to the home in a few days. I was so happy for him. I had been afraid that something bad was going to happen, but it had evidently just been some sort of infection, according to the doctors. I told him that I missed him being at the nursing home. I had resorted to watching reruns of Bonanza with Dad and playing Bridge with Mrs. Kessler. He laughed when I told him of my new pastimes and asked me if I had any peppermints on me. Luckily, I had a couple in my pocket. As he ate the sweet confection, he asked me how my father was getting along.

I took a deep breath and professed, "He is doing fine thanks to you and your crystal."

He calmly continued to swallow the candy and slowly grinned. "So you know about the crystal, do you?" he inquired.

I started to answer, but a nurse burst into the room. "Mr. Harper! It's your father!"

I ran down to the emergency room where I found my worst nightmare. It was my dad, and he was having trouble breathing. My heart sank. This was turning into a deadly game, a rollercoaster ride of pain. I thought those days were over. Dad was doing so much better, yet here we were again in the same old situation. I ran to his side to comfort him.

The doctor yelled to the nurse, "We have to ventilate right now or he's not gonna make it!"

As I backed up to let them work, my gut wrenched in sorrow and pain. I ran out into the lobby to get away from the whole scene. This helpless feeling was all too familiar. Dad was dying, and there was nothing I could do.

As I cried, I thought about Mr. Rent and the crystal. I was desperate. I ran back to his room and told him what was happening.

"I was afraid of this," he said sadly.

I grabbed him by the arm in panic and pleaded for the crystal.

"Only I can use the crystal, young man. Only I know the secrets of its power," he explained.

"Please, Sir, I can't lose him now. I'll do anything. Just please don't let him die!" I begged.

The old man's face wrinkled. He could see that I was at the end of my rope.

"There is one thing! Go get the red blanket! Put it over your father!" he charged.

I didn't ask questions. I drove as fast as I could to the nursing home and grabbed the blanket. When I arrived back at the hospital, the doctor was standing in the lobby.

"We were looking for you," he said calmly. "Your father is sedated and is on the ventilator," he continued. I told the doctor that I wanted to see him.

He was resting quietly when I entered. The sight of the breathing tube made me sick to my stomach. Even though the machine had saved my father many times, I hated it. I took the red blanket and placed it over his torso. I couldn't help but sob as I tucked the blanket around his legs. All the progress-the miracles, they had been in vain. Now he was back to square one, fighting for his life again.

Exhausted, I told the nurses to make sure that the red blanket not be moved. I went out to the lobby and pulled a couple of chairs together and tried to sleep. I said a prayer for my father and for Mr. Rent. I needed the old man to get better. Dad needed him to get better. We needed the crystal in order to have a chance.

I was awakened at 4:00 a.m. by the doctor.

"Mr. Harper! Can I talk to you for a few minutes?" he asked.

I sat up and panicked. I asked if my father was alright and the doctor explained that he was fine.

"It's amazing! I have never seen anything like it before in my twenty years," he exclaimed.

We walked into the room, and there he sat with a saltine cracker in his hand.

"He must have pulled the tube out himself," the doctor stated.

I looked at Dad who took another bite of the cracker.

"What the heck is going on here?" I said in astonishment.

I thought about pinching myself to see if I was dreaming. It was common for me to have dreams about my father eating, talking, and walking, but this was not a dream.

"Dad, can you speak?" I asked.

I figured that perhaps he could talk if he was able to eat. He frowned and shook his head no, but he took the cracker and shoved it into his mouth as if to say, "But I can eat!"

I walked closer to him, and he reached out his hand to me. His fist was closed like he wanted to hand me something. As the doctors and nurses continued to rant and rave, Dad opened his hand and gave me the object.

"Now, where did he get that candy?" the nurse laughed out loud.

I smiled and said, "I think I have an idea."

After celebrating with my father, I went upstairs to visit my old friend. I knew that he had used his magic; somehow he had saved my father. I had to thank him. As I entered his room, the nurse was checking his vitals.

She turned to me and said, "He is resting now. His heart stopped last night, and we had to shock him! He will be out for a while so you might want to come back later."

I wondered how this could be, and it hit me. He had used the crystal. I was sure of it! I asked the nurse when it had happened, and she told me that it was early morning about three or so. That was about the same time that Dad had his miraculous recovery. I started to think about the past weeks and the mysterious things that had occurred. Dad had made such great strides, but Mr. Rent had gotten worse and worse. Perhaps the two happenings were related. Just yesterday, Mr. Rent was looking so much better, and now he had almost died. Then, there was Dad who had come back from certain death and was downstairs eating pudding. Nothing made sense, but the only thing I knew was that when Dad was doing well, Mr. Rent was not. Something had to give.

I walked over to my friend. Even though he was asleep, I took his hand.

"Thank you, Sir," I whispered.

I was getting ready to leave when I noticed a little note by his nightstand. I unfolded the paper to find a message. It was short and read,

"Leave the blanket on your father! It will save him."

From that point on, I made it known to every nurse, doctor, and aide that the red blanket was not to be moved. They probably thought I was crazy, but I was very firm on the subject. I had seen what the crystal could do, so I figured the blanket must have had some similar power. I wasn't taking any chances.

Another week passed, and things were getting back to normal. Dad and Mr. Rent were back at Niletree. Dad was doing great. He was getting around with a walker and playing cards with his fellow patients. He was eating solid foods and was almost back to his old self except he still could not speak. I was grateful, but I longed to hear his voice.

Unfortunately, Mr. Rent was bedfast. He was so weak that he couldn't stand or walk. The doctors all said that it was just a matter of time. I was amazed at how fast death could come. He could barely speak which was the worst thing of all. I missed our conversations. I visited him often and would read the newspaper to him. He would often whisper to me, but it was hard to make out.

"The red blanket! Keep the blanket on him!" he would whisper.

I always assured him that Dad slept under the special quilt.

Dad would accompany me from time to time on my visits to Mr. Rent's room. We would all sit and watch television together. Dad and I didn't want him to feel alone after all that he had done for us. I think the old man enjoyed the company, and it was the least we could do.

Chapter Seven

"Get out and stay out!" Mr. Pyle shouted.

We all heard him and stepped out into the hall to see what was going on. It was a Tuesday which meant that Mad Max probably was involved. The boy ran out of the old man's room holding a toy dart gun, and Mr. Pyle came marching behind him shaking his cane in the air.

"Mr. Pyle, I just wanted to say hello and show you my new gun. Is it like the one you used to shoot in the war?" Max inquired.

The old man stopped and lowered the cane. His face once again turned to stone, but we were all surprised when he knelt down to inspect the toy.

"I had one just like this a long, long time ago," he muttered.

"I figure you had a bunch of guns since you are war hero," the boy added.

The old man's face began to lighten and he put his hand on the boys shoulder. "I'm not much of a hero son, but yes, I did own a few."

Perhaps the little boy reminded him of his little brother or maybe his son, but the old man shocked us all that day when he invited Max into his room to look at old war photos of his friends and weapons.

Amazed, I walked down the hall to listen in on the old man's conversation with the boy. They talked about everything from guns to personal things like family and loss. The little boy sat and stared at the numerous medals that were hanging on the mirror. The old gent talked about his career as a private investigator and all the cases he had solved over the years. He was a fascinating man who had lived through many adventures, and Max loved every minute of the attention and the tales.

Mr. Pyle told of the story about his brother Frank and that deadly day that had haunted him for so long. In a way, Max was therapy for the old fellow. He hadn't talked about those things in a long while, but he seemed comfortable telling them to the little boy. Sometimes it is just easier talking to a child.

"Well, you may as well come in too," the old man said roughly.

He had heard me cough and knew someone was outside his door. I came around the corner to see the two smiling as if they had known I was there for awhile.

"I didn't mean to eavesdrop," I said shyly.

"Have a seat. We were just talking about guns and guy stuff," Max remarked.

I sat and joined the conversation, but mostly, I listened. As the old man told his stories, his eyes would widen as if he was reliving those dreadful days. I told him that I had heard about his heroic deeds and about his brother. He glanced down at the floor to hide his pain but continued to tell his stories.

I interrupted him at one point and asked him a question that I wasn't sure that I should ask. He had mentioned that he had made it to the tank on that day and that he lost his little brother to the gunfire, but he hadn't finished the story.

"Sir, how did you get off that tank and escape after you saved your men?" I asked.

It had been a question that I had wondered about ever since Lena had told me about Mr. Pyle. The old man's eyes once again got wild, and he stopped talking. He walked over to the window, looked to the sky and shook his head. I could tell he was in deep thought, and I was worried that I had opened a new wound. He was apprehensive about answering.

"It was long time ago," he whispered.

"I'm sorry, Sir; it's none of my business." I apologized.

Max walked slowly over to the old man and took his hand. "It's alright, Mr. Pyle."

The old man looked down at the boy and smiled, his heart recognizing the compassion of innocent youth. Mr. Pyle turned to me and once again shook his head, the question still pending in his mind.

He turned again and looked out the window into the deep blue and whispered, "Something saved me, something out of all the smoke and fire, right out of the dark, dusty sky.

Chapter Eight

It was a Friday, and I was going to take my father into town for lunch. His condition had improved so much that I was actually considering taking him home to live with me. Dad loved that idea, he told me. He was gaining fine motor skills and could actually type a little on the laptop that I had bought him. It was a slow process, but he could now tell me that he was hungry or that he needed to use the bathroom by using the keyboard. Any communication was a welcome change.

I put Dad's coat on and wrapped his legs with the red blanket. I put him in the wheelchair and pushed him down the hall. We waved at Mr. Rent as we passed his room, but he didn't see us.

"Would you like anything from town, Sir? How about some candy?" I asked.

He shook his head in decline. It wasn't like him to turn down candy, so I knew he wasn't feeling well.

Dad and I got into my truck, and we were off for the first time in months. Dad stared out the window at the buildings and the people. He was entranced by the scenery of the countryside. As we drove along, I thought about all the things we take for granted in this life. Dad had not seen anything for a long time but the gray walls of his room and that old oak tree that sat outside his window. It inspired me to slow down and enjoy the wonders of this world along with him. That was something that we should all do from time to time.

I wanted to take him somewhere special to eat for lunch, but I let him choose the place. As he took his last bite of the double cheeseburger, we both smiled a satisfied smile. It was still early, so I decided I would take Dad to his old homeplace which was only a few miles down the road. I figured that he had been thinking a lot about the past while he was lying in that hospital bed. He had probably thought that he would never see the outside world again, so I wanted this day to be special.

We got out and I put Dad into the chair. I pushed him by the old pond and up to the little two-bedroom house. As a kid, Dad had taken me to visit grandma every weekend, and it was always hard for me to believe that fifteen children were raised in that tiny home. We sat there in silence for a while. He stared off into space as I skipped rocks on the pond. Nothing had to be said. The silent setting allowed our minds to wonder and remember. It was a great day that I thought would never come.

As I drove him back to the nursing home, we listened to his favorite cassette tape just like we had so many times on past vacations. Every second we spent that day seemed like it was in slow motion. It was a like a wonderful dream for us both, but with life, things come unexpectedly. The thought kept running in my head that joy is a precious thing, but it is limited to the fragile happenings of the world. Happiness does not last forever, so when it comes, one should hold on tight.

Chapter Nine

Nobody could believe their eyes as he limped down the hallway. The fragile, old man who couldn't walk the day before was carrying the nursing home director, Mrs. Blosser, who was unconscious. He laid her down gently on the floor where the other nurses would see her. I rushed to their side and yelled for help. Mr. Rent collapsed beside her. He was drained. He had used every ounce of energy he had left.

The doctor checked the old lady's vitals.

"Call an ambulance!" he ordered.

The nurse and I picked Mr. Rent up and carried him to his room. As I took hold of him, I was surprised at the firmness of his arm. The man couldn't have weighed more than 170 pounds, but he had managed to carry Mrs. Blosser over twenty yards. His eyes opened, but he was so exhausted that all he could muster was, "How is she?"

It turned out that lady had a history of Hypoglycemia and had passed out in Mr. Rent's room. He had pushed his help button but nobody had come. The old man had taken it upon himself to help the woman, to save her. The doctor said that her sugar had bottomed out and that time had been of the essence. The gentleman in room 205 was a hero to everyone at Niletree. Of course, he had already been a hero to me, and it just increased my respect for him.

Mrs. Kessler had been standing in the hall observing all the action. I hadn't visited her in days, so I walked down to say hello.

"Hi, Mrs. Kessler, how are you today?" I said gleefully.

"Who are you? Do I know you?" she said in a confused tone.

It appeared that perhaps the sweet old lady had a memory problem.

I commented, "My name is Mr. Harper. I visited you a while back. We played cards."

She studied my face and said, "Oh yes, I'm sorry! I can't remember things at times."

I smiled and told her that it was okay. I noticed that her name on the whiteboard once again said "Mrs. Ressler" so I informed her about it.

"Oh, that aide can't spell worth anything," she said in disgust.

She pulled the marker out of her pocket and made the necessary corrections.

She laughed and said, "One of these days I'm going to forget who I really am and become Mrs. Ressler."

We both giggled at her clever remark.

I went into her room and sat down in the rocking chair. She poured me some tea and asked if I wanted a cookie. We sat and talked for a few minutes before she mentioned our old friend in room 205. We had discussed the old man at different times, but that day proved to be different. The story I got on that day was a long one.

"I met him in the great flood of 1947," she said.

"Oh, he was handsome back in those days!" she added.

I was surprised because she had never mentioned this to me before. She had told me that she didn't really know him, but now I was finding out more, the truth. The old lady's memory was obviously diminishing, but on this day, she told every detail like it had just happened yesterday.

She told of the flood that had threatened the local area and of a man who had been a newspaper reporter from out of town. He had come to the town to do a story on the flooding that was devastating the region. He had been in his late twenties at the time and had apparently been a real ladies' man.

"All the girls went crazy over him, including me," she giggled.

She went on to tell me about how he wrote an article about the terrible disaster and how the article had inspired people from all around the United States.

"People came by the hundreds to help rebuild our little town, and it was all because of him," she added.

As she continued to tell the story about my old friend, I could picture it all in my head.

"I was in love with him, but he didn't love me back! There was only one girl for him," she said sadly.

"I can't remember her name right off, but I recall that she was a local girl and a widow," she continued.

She kept talking into the night about Mr. Rent's accomplishments as a journalist and about his love life. The old box of newspapers made perfect sense to me now. He simply collected his own articles. I laughed at how simple the explanation had been.

As she wrapped up the epic story, she said that he had only stayed in the area for a few weeks before going back to the city. She only saw him two more times. That was when he was visiting the widow and her kids.

"I always thought that it was strange for him to fall for a woman with that many kids," she laughed.

"Maybe that's why he didn't come back," I joked.

I told Mrs. Kessler that it had been a pleasure. I was getting tired, and I still had to go visit my father.

"Check my name again on the way out," the old lady added.

I peeked out at the white board and concluded, "Looks good, Mrs. Kessler! Goodnight!"

Chapter Ten

We all sat in the lobby and watched it over the big screen television. You never expect things like that to happen to anyone you know, but it was here and now, and we all had to face it. A child had been taken, abducted from a bus stop on North Avenue in the downtown section. Rolling Hills was a safe place for most, but even small towns have their demons, and we knew in most cases that these things did not end well. Mr. Pyle knew this to be true better than all of us.

Working as a detective had been an exciting job but eye opening to the dangers of society and people. There were bad people, infamous villains who preyed upon the weak and upon little children. These were the worst kinds of people, and Mr. Pyle had devoted his life to putting them behind bars. For 30 years, Robert Pyle had gone up against some of the most venomous killers and never been afraid, never scared to die, never afraid at all, but today fear came. On that day there was pure evil in the air, and he had a gut feeling that there was something more to it.

When they flashed the picture of the little boy on the screen, Mrs. Kessler cried out and Mrs. Blosser hung her head. It was like a nightmare, like an unbelievable dream. The picture was of Max and his mother at his last birthday party, his smile so haunting as if he were already a ghost.

Lena had not come to work, so we knew that it was true. Lena worked every day, the dayshift and never missed.

"Oh, poor Lena!" I thought.

Max was all she had in this world, and some evil thing had taken him. There was a helpless feeling throughout the nursing home; our beloved Max was gone. I looked to Mr. Rent who was staring at the wall and I reflected on his miracles, but not even he could help this time. The world is just too big, even in a small town.

Mr. Pyle stood with an evident tear rolling down his cheek, a rigid look on his face. As he slowly walked to his room, I thought he was broken once again. Everything the old man loved would eventually leave, die, but not Max. Max was special with his little laugh, his bright eyes, and his caring heart. This was not acceptable to me and evidently, not acceptable to Robert Pyle.

He dressed slowly as I entered his room, carefully placing his remaining medals on his chest. It was some sort of decorated military suit. He had one last battle in him I suppose.

"What are you doing, Mr. Pyle?" I asked.

He looked in the mirror and straightened his tie, my words going through him.

"Not again, never again," he muttered.

I knew exactly what he was saying, where he was going, and for a second, I thought about calling the nurses. He was an old man and what could he do, but somehow I knew that he must try.

"Sir, I am going with you. I'll drive," I added.

There was no way I could let him go alone in his fragile state. He went to an old cedar box at the foot of his bed and opened it. He grabbed a musty cloth and placed it on his bed. As he unfolded it, the knife was exposed.

"It belonged to Frank," he said.

He placed it on his belt and grabbed his hat, and we were off. We snuck out of the place without anyone even noticing. As I pulled the car around to pick him up, I had to beep my horn to bring him back from a trance-like state. He was obviously thinking and thinking hard.

Mr. Pyle knew every lowlife in every sleazy bar in town, and that is where we had to start our search. There were only three watering holes in the area, and those were our only chances. We were a sight to see, an old officer and a young businessman with khaki pants. We didn't exactly fit in, but we had a job to do and we were going to do it. We had to for Max.

Chapter Eleven

We stopped by a local gas station to grab some drinks, and Mr. Pyle bought a newspaper. As I took a sip, he ripped a page out of the paper. It was the picture of Max that had been seen on television. We would need it to show to people just like those detectives did in the movies. As we drove, Mr. Pyle stared at the picture and fought back a tear. His love for the boy had grown, and he knew that we were his only hope.

The police are hard working, good guys, but nobody really cares about the ones you love, not like you do. The police deal with it every day. They have to accept the heartache of a case gone wrong, but they deal with it. Mr. Pyle knew that if something happened to Max that his life would be over as well. When you feel love, I guess you get greedy for it. Robert Pyle loved the boy, and that was the bottom line. He had opened his heart one last time and would not settle for anything less than his boy Max. Only a happy ending would do, but I knew the truth. Happy endings are rare in the situation we were facing, and I felt sorry for the old man. Still, it did not hurt to try even though it was a long shot.

We had asked every person in the first two bars and nobody had seen the boy. I began to think that the demon could have been from out of town, taking Max to another state, another place. My heart sank as we got into the car to go to the last bar.

As we stopped at a red light, I looked over at an elderly gentleman who was crossing the street. He was slightly bent over and was moving slow. I thought to myself that the old chap looked like Mr. Rent, but I knew that was impossible. I figured that most old people resemble each other in many ways, so I dismissed the thought and continued to our sleazy destination.

We entered, and the bartender smirked. "Well, well, well, Robert Pyle," the man said.

He knew Mr. Pyle and the old man smiled. "It's been a long time, Hank," Pyle replied.

He introduced me then sat down for a drink. Mr. Pyle talked to the man for a few minutes, but he knew nothing. We walked around the entire place asking every drunk if they had seen the boy, but nobody had seen Max or even heard about the abduction. The old man hung his head as reality was setting in, and he knew that it was over. We had made an attempt, and that is more than most people would have done. Then I saw it. It shined brightly as the club lights glistened off it. It was hanging on the mirror behind the bar just like it had hung proudly on Mr. Pyle's wall. It was the medal, the same medal that the old man had given Max.

"Look, Sir! It's yours, isn't it?" I exclaimed.

Mr. Pyle smiled and said, "No, ha, no, that belongs to Max," he laughed.

We asked the bartender where he had gotten the medal, and it was just as we had hoped.

"Oh, Philips gave me that. He is a real oddball. He had a tab in here and that guy never has any money! So, he gave me that and I figured it was worth at least the fifty bucks he owed me," Hank laughed.

Mr. Pyle asked him about the man and where we could find him. The answer was just what we wanted to hear.

"Phillips lives just around the corner on North Central in the old Dodd Place," he said.

Mr. Pyle and I smiled at each other and exhausted an excited breath. As I got up to call the police, the old man took my shoulder.

"No, Son, we have to do this alone."

I didn't understand. He went on to inform me that he was once in the same situation, and he had called the police for assistance. It ended in a hostage situation, and it took the life of a small boy, all because the police took over.

I won't make that mistake again. We need surprise, sneak him right out of there," the old man said intently.

I shook my head as I tried to convince myself that we were doing the right thing. Perhaps it was the pain in the old man's eyes or the fact that he was alone in the world. My heart ached for him, and my brain reacted accordingly. Down deep I knew he was right. We could not take the chance of alerting the police or the media. We could not risk a hostage situation. Mr. Pyle tipped his hat to a young lady at the bar and we left to find our boy, our friend, Max.

Chapter Twelve

Back at the nursing home the director was frantic at finding out that Mr. Pyle was missing as well as Mr. Rent, who was in no condition to be on his feet. Lena had come in earlier to check and see if Max had wandered off again and perhaps found his way to the home. She had been disappointed when she found that Mr. Pyle was missing and that Max was nowhere to be found. She had gone and talked to Mr. Rent, for she had heard the whispers, the rumors about his magic. The old man had been sickly, but listened and had comforted her. Lena was a good woman and didn't deserve this added heartbreak, this torturous nightmare.

Mr. Rent must have listened to her pleads because he too was now missing. The director had called the police. We were all fugitives, just like the demon. Even though the administration at the home was angry and scolded the nurses and the aides, everyone was happy that we were gone. They all knew what we were doing, and they loved the little boy as we did. They smirked as they received their punishments. They smiled for us, for Max.

As we drove to the place, we listened to the radio about the abduction. A witness had seen the color of the car that the demon drove. It was a red van. I thought that it was appropriate for the devil to drive, a Satan car used for stealing babies. When we pulled around the corner, we saw the place. It was a bad neighborhood, and the building looked almost abandoned with its dark entryway and broken windows. Above the door were the words "Dodd Manor." I began thinking that this was a really bad idea, but then I pictured Max in that place, sitting in the darkness. My heart began to pound with half fear and half anger.

Mr. Pyle informed me that it would be best to go through the backdoor. There were no cars in sight so we were hopeful that we could get in and out without any trouble. Mr. Pyle carefully pried open a back window with his knife and I crawled in to unlock the door. As I entered, I could smell it, like rotten eggs. I opened the door and could tell that Mr. Pyle smelled it too because he looked away from me. Even I knew that bad smells were bad news. I got a sick feeling thinking about the terrible possibilities. I shook it out of my head and proceeded to the bottom of the stairs with Mr. Pyle at my side.

Holding his knife tightly, he took one step up and the wood creaked. We looked at each other and knew it was going to be hard to sneak to the upstairs bedrooms, but it had to be done. Another step brought another sound, a low moan. The moan came from up to the right, and Mr. Pyle held the knife out in front of him as if to pounce on whatever we were about to encounter. Step by step, my heart beat faster. I was terrified at what we might see, what might be around the corner.

We made it to the first door, and Mr. Pyle quietly opened it to find nothing but an old, torn bed. Then, a loud sound that nearly made me faint: it was a lonely dove that had taken off from the bed post to the window which was already shattered into a thousand pieces on the floor. As we continued to the next bedroom, we heard it again, a lonely whimper. I opened the door, and there he was sitting in the corner with his arms wrapped tightly around his knees. The boy looked up to see Mr. Pyle smiling, and he ran to hug him. He clung onto the old man and nearly made him lose his balance. I put my arms around Max and told him that we were going to get him out of there and that everything was going to be okay.

I bent over to pick up the knife that Mr. Pyle had dropped and glimpsed out the window to see it. The red van, the devil car, pulled into the driveway.

"He's back! Mr. Pyle, He's back!" I whispered.

We heard the front door open and shut, and Max began to cry. Mr. Pyle took his hand and put it over the boy's mouth and winked at him to reassure him. Even though we knew we were in danger, we had to think, stay calm and find a way out.

We looked around the room and realized that we were trapped. Mr. Pyle told Max to go back to the corner while he stooped down behind the bed. I propped myself up behind the door; it was the only place left to hide. We didn't say a word, but we knew what we had to do. I would have to take him down, and Mr. Pyle would have to come out from behind the bed and use the knife. It was the only way.

The demon entered the room and walked over to Max. The boy played his part well, not to give us away. He kicked the child in the stomach and cursed at him, and I saw Mr. Pyle's head bobble up for a second. It was time for us to make our move, but then the man pulled the gun out from the back of his belt. He waved it at the boy to intimidate, to show his power. I knew at that moment that something bad was going to happen, and I thought about my life, the way I was living. I wondered if God would see us through this nightmare. Then, the man turned to the door where I was hiding. I was breathing harder and knew that I had been exposed. He walked over, pointing his gun at me.

"Won't you come out and play with us?" he laughed.

I stepped out from behind the door. Me, in my khaki pants, Mr. Businessman, I stepped out.

"Let the boy go!" I pleaded.

The man walked toward the window and raised his gun a little higher to aim at my head. The plan had changed. I would try to talk to the demon, keep his attention while Mr. Pyle snuck. They were taught that in the Army, to sneak, to cut. I saw the old man slowly rise up, and I kept talking to him.

"It's not worth it. Just put the gun down and let us go," I continued.

The demon took his hand and ran it through his hair. I noticed the scars on his wrist and red blotches all over his arms. He reached to his face and scratched it hard bringing blood. It was clear that the man was insane which reinforced my thoughts that we were not getting out of this alive.

The old man crept slowly toward his target, but it happened. The old house's rotten floor exposed our plan and the man turned. Now the maniac faced us all. He took his hand again to his face and sliced new flesh bringing more blood, dripping heavily now. Then he slowly took the gun and pointed it at the boy. He began to laugh wildly, and Mr. Pyle let out a war scream. He no longer thought of himself, only to protect the child. The old man ran and jumped on top of Max to take it, to cover.

It all seemed sublime as the gun went off, and my mind flashed back to a summer day in my backyard and the old tackling dummy that my father had made for me. I had hit it so hard that on occasion it had torn and exploded into pieces of stuffed cotton.

"When you hit someone, unleash all of your fury, all of your pain! When you hit them, make sure they don't get back up!"

The words of my father, my football coach, rang in my ear. I pictured my dad lying in that bed, the stroke, the suffering, and my fear subsided. At that moment, there was just a peaceful madness. I glimpsed at my friends and then back at the demon. I stared through him as if persuading him to shoot. There was no fear, just anger and disgust.

The bullet had hit Mr. Pyle in the lower back and I saw the blood soak through his jacket. My rage overtook me. Then I ran! "Unleash it! Let it go!"

The demon turned to fire at me. The bullet missed me; somehow it missed me. Then another shot, but the gun jammed.

I hit him low and hard as we both took flight into the wall. His head hurled into the furnace making a scraping sound. The gun laid smoking on the floor and the devil next to it unconscious. I quickly picked it up, but it burnt my hand. As I knelt to examine it, the barrel was slightly bent and the tip was practically melted shut.

I ran over to Mr. Pyle who was still bleeding profusely, and I told him to hold on. I showed Max how to apply pressure to the wound using my shirt and grabbed my cell phone.

"We did it, Frank! We finally did it!" the old man whispered.

Max held Mr. Pyle while I dialed 911 for an ambulance. The ordeal was over, and we had survived, at least for the moment.

I went over to the demon and examined him. His head was cut badly and still bleeding from the blow of the furnace. I thought for a second that I was lucky that the bullet had missed me, so close to death. Beside him was the gun, still smoking, and I thought to myself how bizarre for it to malfunction in that manner. I had owned several guns in my lifetime and none had ever had a meltdown. I looked out the window and up into the sky. I said a prayer for Mr. Pyle and thanked God for helping us. It was evident that he had been there that day.

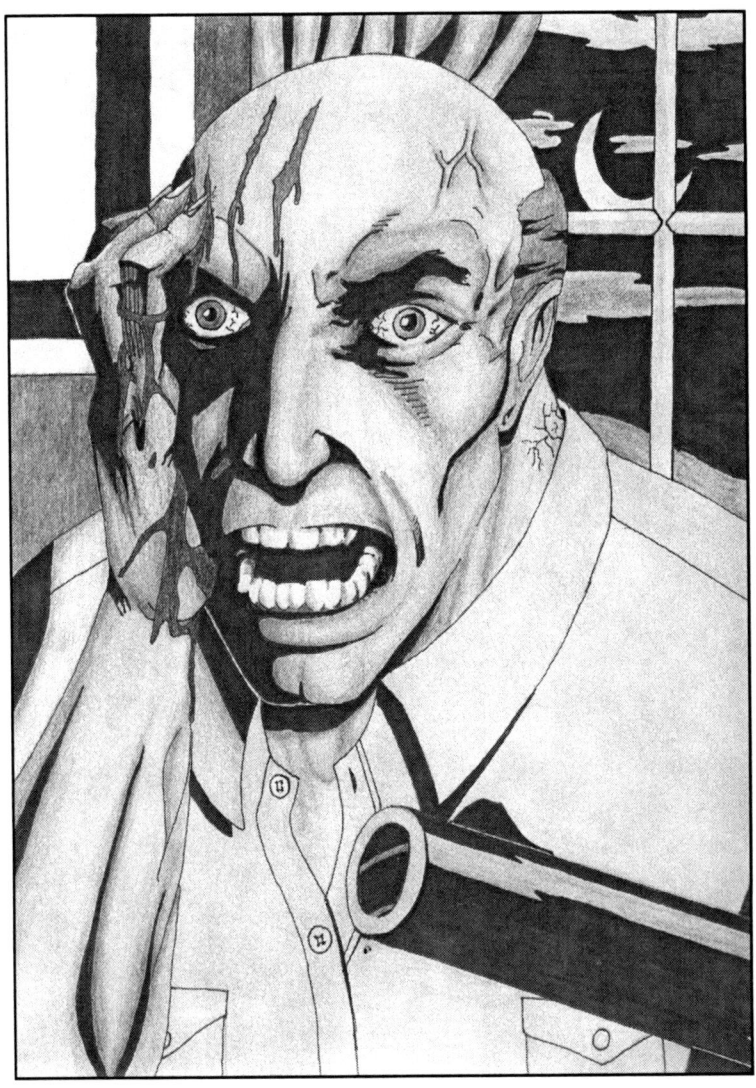

As I finally took a breath, I noticed it. The medal, Max's medal, was lying on the windowsill. I once again looked to the sky and smiled. How it got there no longer mattered in my mind. We were alive. I thought about my father and couldn't wait to get back to him. I took the medal over to Max. The boy kissed the old man and placed it proudly on his chest with the others. As the child cried, he whispered, "You are a hero, Mr. Pyle, always have been!"

Chapter Thirteen

Lena ran to Max and squeezed him hard. She looked at me and her eyes told the story of constant tears and loss of hope. She hugged me and gave me a big kiss and asked about Mr. Pyle. I informed her that he was in the hospital and that it didn't look good. The old man's spine had been shattered by the bullet and although he would survive, the doctor had told me that he would not walk again. The old man smiled as he had gone into surgery and told me not to worry. It was obvious that he was at peace. Max was alive, and that was all that mattered, alive and well reunited with his mother at last. It was a good feeling, one of the only good feelings I had experienced in awhile. As Max and his mother left to go check on their old friend, I hurried to my father's room. He looked over at me, and his eyes widened as if to say, "Where have you been?"

I laughed and said, "Pop, did you miss me?"

He replied with a smile. He seemed weaker and paler, but he was still able to move about some. It seemed that he would have a good day and then several bad days in a row. He was still better than before, and I was thankful.

The newspapers and television stations came for the story, and I had to be in the spotlight which was not a good thing. I was a private person, and I just wanted to be left alone, but the media was relentless. So I gave my interviews, always commenting on the real hero, Mr. Pyle.

Within a couple of days, the madness was over, and it was time to concentrate on my father again. I once again found myself in a funky depression about the stroke, so I sat down and watched some television. It had been nice to forget about the little room, the bed, the stroke, even for a little while. Even though it had been under terrible circumstances, I had escaped from the nursing home for a short time and hadn't dwelled on his illness. Now I was back in the room, back where I could see his agony and it hurt. Even though he had improved, he was still having problems with his breathing and balance. With every setback, that old familiar dullness in my heart would bring me down to a low-level, depressed state.

Mr. Rent had found his way back to the home as well. He claimed that he simply went out to hang fliers that he had made of the missing boy. I wondered if he had been the old man that I had seen cross the street. I wondered if he had followed us and helped us somehow with his magic. I pictured the gun, the melted gun, in my mind and wondered. He was a wizard of some sort, a healer, a hero. My mind didn't want to accept that illogical thought, but my heart told me that it was true. I had seen too much, too many impossible things in the last little while to ignore the notion.

I was relieved that everything had turned out alright and that Mr. Rent was home. When Dad fell asleep, Mr. Rent and I went to visit the old man at the hospital. Lena and Max were sitting in the waiting room playing cards.

"Why don't you guys go get some rest? I will stay for a while." I stated.

Max looked up at me and shook his head no. The boy realized what the old man had done, the sacrifice that he had made, and he was not leaving. I understood completely and it said something about the boy's character to do so.

The doctor came out and told me that we could go in for just a moment. Mr. Pyle needed his rest, and we knew it. Mr. Rent and I entered the room, and the old man smiled. He was groggy from the medication, but nonetheless, tried to sit up a bit to talk.

"I saw you on TV, young man," he laughed.

I grinned and told him that it would be his turn as soon as he got out of the hospital. I took his hand and asked him if it hurt, and he just shrugged.

"It will take more than a bullet to slow me down, but we did it, didn't we?" he said ruggedly.

Mr. Rent limped over to him and put his hand on the old man's shoulder and said, "You did well, Robert, very well." Mr. Pyle flinched as if a bit apprehensive and stared at Mr. Rent. His eyes were getting heavy and his speech more groggy.

"You, you were there. I saw you there, there at the window," the old man stuttered.

Mr. Rent cleared his throat and looked at me with a crooked smile. "I think our friend is sleepy. We better leave and let him rest."

I wasn't sure what Mr. Pyle was talking about, but I remembered the medal on the windowsill and seeing the old man at the crossing. Mr. Rent had been missing at the same time and I had suspected, but dismissed it.

Mr. Pyle closed his eyes, still chattering on about Frank, Mr. Rent, the war, ideas that were obviously brought on by his medication. I bent over and patted the old man on his chest and told him to get some rest, and his eyes opened slightly.

"There at the window, look there at the window," the old man muttered.

I turned and looked at the window behind me, but there was nothing to be seen. Mr. Pyle pointed to the window and closed his eyes again.

"The window, right out of the dark sky, right out of the dark, dusty sky," he whispered, and the old man slept.

As we walked out, my mind was clouded with possibilities and doubts. I looked at my friend Mr. Rent, trying to figure it out. Lena walked over to us and gave us each a hug. I knelt down beside Max who was now asleep on two hospital chairs and touched his head. I ran my hands through his hair and wondered how anyone could ever hurt a child. I recalled the old house, the demon, and tried to block out what might have happened if we hadn't found the boy. I tried to block out what might have already happened to him. He was already changed, and that was clear. It had been a harsh reality, a stealing of innocence for all of us and especially Max.

Mr. Rent stood beside me and commented, "It's a cruel world out there. There are many demons to fight. Be thankful that we won. The good guys don't always win."

I nodded and we turned to Lena. She looked so tired with her hair frazzled and her darkened eyes. Still, she seemed strong, stronger than the woman we knew before.

As we turned again to leave, she ran and put an arm around each of us and cried, "I know one thing! I'm glad I have the good guys on my side."

Chapter Fourteen

I woke up one night after a terrible nightmare about my father. In the dream, he was still unable to move or walk. He was completely surrounded by flames as I was trying to reach him. It was one of those weird episodes where all the sounds were muffled. I could actually feel the heat of the fire. It was a hopeless feeling that had left me with a pounding headache when I awoke. I was drenched in sweat and my heart was beating rapidly. The nausea from the pain in my head overcame me causing me to be sick right there in my bed.

I had dreamt often over the last few weeks. There were the nightmares about the demon, but most were good dreams about my father walking and talking. This dream had been different. So many strange things had been happening lately that I wondered if it had been some sort of warning.

As I sat with Mr. Rent and read the magazine article, his breathing was somewhat labored. It reminded me of the sound that my father had often made when he was bedfast. It was a horrible sound that I did not want to hear. Time continued taking its toll on my old friend.

My head began hurting once again after reading all of the fine print. Mr. Rent was talking more than usual on this day, so I decided that I would bring up the box of articles on the floor.

"I heard you were quite the journalist in your day, Sir," I professed.

"That was a long time ago, young man," he replied.

He pointed to the box of papers and added, "That was my life all written down!"

I knelt down and dug through the box.

"I would love to read some of these sometime, Sir," I hinted.

As I reached the bottom of his treasures, I noticed a blue velvet-like bag. I picked it up and peeked inside. There was a faint glow. It was the crystal.

"Be very careful with that, young man," Mr. Rent said calmly.

I remarked, "So this is the famous crystal! What is it really, Sir?"

The old man smirked and shook his head, "In time, young man, in time!"

As I placed the crystal back in the box, I realized that my headache was completely gone.

"That's funny, my head stopped hurting," I said in surprise.

The old man chuckled with delight as if I had just told a joke. I wondered if the crystal had something to do with it, but just like that, Mr. Rent closed his eyes for a nap. I started to take a few of the newspaper articles with me, but I figured that I had better wait until my old friend was awake.

I pulled the covers up and tucked him in and whispered, "Talk to you soon, Sir. God bless you."

I went to Dad's room to help him with his daily strength training. I pushed him hard to do his exercises because there were days when he just wanted me to go away and leave him alone.

"Come on, Pop! It's time to get physical," I would order.

Dad, who would have rather just watched television, would put his hand up in disgust.

I would just smile at him and say, "Well, Dad, I didn't know you knew sign language!"

He loved to give me a hard time, but always did whatever I suggested. He knew that it was for his own good.

After our workout, Dad always wanted a cup of coffee. I think of all the things that he had missed out on, he had missed his morning coffee the most. I helped him back into bed and covered him up with the red blanket. I always wrapped his legs up extra tight. Even though he could walk a little, he was still very shaky. I went down the hall and filled our cups. I even delivered a cup to Mrs. Kessler who was sitting in her chair crocheting a throw.

I stuck my head in her room and said, "You need to fix your name!"

It was becoming a common joke between the two of us, and we would always make sure the aides heard our comments.

"Those darn aides can't spell worth a dime," she chuckled.

I gave her the coffee and went back to the desk to get the cups that I had poured earlier.

I entered Dad's room and placed the coffee on his portable table. I rolled the stand around and placed it over his lap. Before I could put in the cream and sugar, he reached for his cup. Still a little clumsy, his hand shook as he lifted it from the table.

"Dad, let my help you," I uttered.

It was too late. The scalding hot coffee spilled all over his legs. I waited for him to flinch, moan, or something, but he just sat there. We looked at each other in amazement. All of the hot liquid had fallen on the red blanket, so I picked it up carefully. It was dry, and there wasn't a stain anywhere. The coffee itself had drained down to the floor where it had formed in a little puddle.

"Well, Mr. Rent said that it would protect you, but I didn't know that included hot coffee," I tried to joke.

Dad looked intently at the blanket and took it to his mouth. He knew that the blanket was special, and he acted like he thought maybe the magic would help heal his speech just like it had his limbs. I wrapped Dad's legs up even tighter and kissed him goodbye. It had been a long day already.

As I put my coat on, I said, "You will talk again, Dad! I promise!"

Chapter Fifteen

Mr. Jim was one of the patients that lived on the other side of the hospital complex. He never spoke to anyone, and I had figured that he was simply unable to speak perhaps from a stroke or other illness. He was always getting into trouble with the nurses. He loved to jump out from behind the door and scare the other patients. He was quite the character, and his favorite pastime was taking pictures of his unsuspecting victims. He had the photos plastered all over his room and loved to show them off to any visitor who was game.

He communicated by hand motions and a very loud grunting sound that was actually kind of scary. Mr. Jim was not a big guy. His small frame could barely hold up the antique camera that he used to catch his masterful images. He was one of those people that you know you shouldn't laugh at, but he made it so hard not to smile.

One day, I was walking down the hallway to the snack room when he leapt out from behind the water fountain and almost gave me a coronary. The camera flashed, and I became a new member on his wall of shame. He grunted with delight as I rubbed my eyes from the extremely bright light. He grabbed my hand and led me to his room to show me all of his works of art. It was a hilarious collage of all the nurses and doctors that had worked at Niletree over the past year. I wondered to myself just where my face would fit in the mix.

As I admired the wall of shame, he closed the door behind us.

"Sit down!" he whispered.

My mouth dropped to the floor. I had been there for some time now and never heard more than a grunt out of him. His articulation was perfect as he continued to speak to me.

"Sorry for all the secrecy, but it's for the best," he exclaimed.

I didn't know what he was talking about, but I played along.

"Oh, it's okay, Mr. Jim! You just surprised me," I commented.

The old jokester had really pulled one off by fooling everyone, I thought to myself. I asked him why he had never spoken to me before, and he laughed.

"You may not believe me, but I was unable to speak at one time!" he said.

He went on to tell me that he had suffered a stroke several months back that had taken his speech. His left arm and leg had been slightly paralyzed, but he had regained his strength after rehabilitation.

"My speech never came back, that is, until just after he came to help," he continued to whisper.

"Why aren't you telling everyone? This is something that you should celebrate," I said.

He looked at me and said, "For the same reason that you haven't told anyone about the gentlemen in room 205."

I got deathly quiet. How did he know?

"We used to work together a long time ago," Mr. Jim stated.

"He always spoke of how beautiful this area was and how friendly the people were here. Rolling Hills sounded like the perfect little town," he explained.

I sat there quietly, not wanting to miss a thing. As Mr. Jim continued his story, he gazed out the window into the darkness as if in a nostalgic trance.

"I used to love to sit on my porch with a cold glass of tea and watch the sun sink down into those majestic mountains," he said sadly.

I looked out the window and felt his pain. I too loved the outdoors and the mesmerizing view from my back patio. It must be hard living at Niletree with such limited accommodations.

He turned his head back around and returned to the conversation.

"So, on my fifty-ninth birthday, I retired and left the hustle and bustle of the big city. I had remembered all of the wonderful things that my friend had said about Rolling Hills. I figured that it was as good of a place as any to spend the rest of my days. I packed and never looked back," he laughed.

I started to comment, but we were interrupted by Lena who was passing out dinner trays. Mr. Jim clammed up and gave me a little wink.

"Well, I'm going to check on Dad. Thanks for listening, Sir." I winked back.

As I exited the room, I wondered just how it had come to be that the old friends had ended up in the same little town and the same nursing home. I knew that there had to be more to the story, but I decided not to pry. I respected my new acquaintances and knew that they would tell me in time.

Chapter Sixteen

Dad had seemed rather depressed on Sunday when I had gone to visit, so I decided to take action. I couldn't blame him; sitting in that room had to be torture for someone who had been so active in his life. Even an earlier visit from Max hadn't cheered him up. I sat and brainstormed for an hour before the idea finally hit me. I got in my truck and drove to my house. I grabbed two big cardboard boxes and filled them with my father's treasures. He was forgetting how special his life had been, so I took it upon myself to remind him.

I waited until lunch time to do my decorating. I knew Dad would be out of the room for at least a half an hour, so it was the perfect time. He would be so surprised when he returned. As I carried the boxes from my vehicle, I noticed Mr. Jim going into room 205. When I walked by the room, I peeked in to see the two old friends embrace. It warmed my heart to see that Mr. Rent had someone else besides me to watch over him. I had been very busy with my dad and hadn't been able to spend much time with the old man.

I entered Dad's room and started unpacking the trophies. There were so many it was hard to count, and there were just as many plaques. I figured that football had made my father the happiest over the years, so I thought that the awards would serve as good motivation for him.

Of course, he loved for people to brag on his many accomplishments, so it wouldn't hurt to remind everyone.

As I placed the last trophy on top of the television, Lena popped her head in and said, "Wow! Your dad was the man!"

I laughed and replied, "He still is, just not as fast."

As I looked around the room, I could hear the cheers from the crowd. My father had been one of the best football players in the country. He had broken records in high school and college and earned the nickname "Iron Man." As a boy, his old teammates would tell me that it was almost impossible to catch him let alone tackle him. It had always made me so proud to hear about the glory-day stories that my father and his friends would tell.

As I searched through the boxes for the remaining newspaper clippings, I found the one article that I would not be hanging on the wall. It read, "Iron Man Falls!" It told of how my father was in his last year of college football and how he had injured his knee. It had been one of the lowest points in his life. Football was gone. His dreams of playing after college faded, so he had turned to teaching and politics. He had to be known. He had to be a success.

Dad entered the room and smiled. He placed his walker in the corner and inspected every award. He picked up one of the trophies and dusted it off. He limped from wall to wall admiring my work. He smiled and thanked me with a hug.

"Maybe this will get you a woman, Pop," I joked.

He grinned and tried to laugh, but only a loud muffled sound came out. We sat there for the rest of the afternoon reading old newspaper clippings about how the Iron Man of Rolling Hills had conquered the football world. It was a wonderful day of reminiscing and reflection. It was obvious that it had provided some motivation to Dad when he almost fell out of bed demonstrating how he used to forearm a would-be tackler. I was glad that my plan had worked. As he held a trophy to his heart, he drifted off to dream about those wonderful days when things were simple.

Mr. Rent hadn't been out of bed for days, and I was getting concerned. The bed was often a death sentence at Niletree Nursing Home. It seemed that once a patient became immobile, more health problems were sure to follow. I asked Lena about his daily routine, and she informed me that he was in bed for most of the day with only thirty minutes of bedside therapy. I asked her if it would be okay for me to do some additional therapy with him as well. She told me to simply close the door and to keep it to myself.

"It would do him good, but it's against the rules. But what they don't know won't hurt them," she whispered.

I smuggled the dumbbells into his room using my gym bag.

"How are you today, Sir," I said cheerfully.

He looked tired and run down, but I knew it was simply from a lack of circulation. I took the weights out of my bag and lifted them up to show him.

He jokingly asked, "Are you going to be working out in here?"

I didn't say a word. I took one of the dumbbells and put it in his right hand. He smirked at me and gave me ten reps with no problem. He switched hands and did another ten reps with his left arm.

"I'm not going to let you do it, Sir," I stated in a serious tone.

He asked me what I was talking about and leaned over to make direct eye contact. "I'm not going to let you die!"

He now had a grim look on his face.

"Everybody dies, young man," he said.

I didn't respond. Instead I told him to give me another ten reps. He shook his head in disbelief and did as I wished. It was evident that he wouldn't help himself, but he would do what others asked of him. I figured I could use that fact to help him to get better.

After the workout, I poured him a glass of water. As I handed him the drink, I noticed that he was staring at me in a different manner.

"You have turned out to be a wonderful person, young man," he said.

All of sudden he got really quiet like he had said something wrong. He lifted his glass to his lips in order to hide his humility. The statement had been heartfelt, and I had appreciated the loving words. But there was something odd about the compliment. I hadn't known the old man long, yet the phrase had sounded like we had known each other forever.

"Thank you, Sir. I think you are pretty wonderful yourself," I said playfully.

I told Mr. Rent that I would be coming in for a workout every day, and he didn't think that was wonderful at all. I decided that I would bring Dad along and kill two birds with one stone. So, as my father and Mr. Rent pumped iron, I sat in my chair and counted the reps. I would tell jokes or read the paper as they completed their exercise routines. I bought them each ankle weights as well, so they could strengthen their leg muscles. Dad had begun walking better so I figured that I would return the red blanket to Mr. Rent. If it did have some sort of magic in it, then Mr. Rent needed it more at the moment. When I tried to give it back to him though, he told me very sternly to make sure that I kept it on my Dad's legs. I didn't argue with him. It was his blanket and he must have known something that I didn't.

I couldn't help but notice how Mr. Rent would stare at my father. There was a connection there that I couldn't explain. Even though Dad couldn't speak, it was like they communicated by other means. When I couldn't understand what my father wanted, Mr. Rent could step in and interpret.

"You father is very special, young man," Mr. Rent exclaimed.

The statement came from out of nowhere. We were all just sitting there drinking our post-workout water.

"He was one heck of a football player in his day!" he continued.

I looked at Dad who was smiling from ear to ear.

"How do you know, Sir?" I inquired.

The old man avoided my eye contact but replied, "Oh everyone knows that. I was a journalist remember? It was my job to listen for stories!"

I smiled and told the old man that when he got a little better that I would take him to my father's room to show him the awards. Mr. Rent agreed and stated his favorite saying, "In time, young man, in time."

Chapter Seventeen

Thursdays used to be my bowling night, but with my new second home, things had changed. I now spent my Thursdays with a new group of individuals, and the new game was poker. There was Mrs. Kessler who supplied the tea and Mr. Jim who often had an ace up his sleeve. Even Mr. Pyle and Max would sit in on occasion. Then, there was my father who considered himself a poker expert, and me, who lost at least twenty bucks each week.

We would play for hours and talk about everything from sports to politics. One night we got on the topic of the old man in room 205. Mrs. Kessler started the conversation by asking me how the old chap was doing. I informed her that he was about the same.

"Such a shame about him!" she exclaimed. "He can heal everyone, but can't heal himself," she continued.

I guess the look on my face indicated my confusion. I looked at Mr. Jim who started laughing.

"Yes, she knows about it too," he giggled.

I started to wonder just how many people the old man had helped. I asked the old lady about her story, and she was more than happy to oblige.

"It happened the day after I saw him holding that crystal over your father," she began.

She continued to tell us that she had fallen in the shower and had injured her hip.

"Oh, I could barely walk," she said.

The nurses had placed her in bed and called the hospital to arrange for an X-Ray. While she waited on the ambulance, she had a visitor.

"He brought me a blanket," she giggled.

She had thought it was strange, but she accepted it to be polite. He had covered her legs and hip with it and told her not to take it off.

"It was amazing! The pain went away immediately," she exclaimed.

The old lady smiled and concluded, "He healed me just like he healed Mr. Jim and your father!"

I sat there stunned and confused. Why couldn't the old gentleman heal himself? He had healed Mr. Jim and given him his speech back. It was time to talk to Mr. Rent about the crystal, the blanket, and my father.

I entered Mr. Rent's room with a determined look on my face. He was sitting there looking at an old scrapbook. His pale complexion and skinny frame made him look like a skeleton. Even though we were all trying to keep him, he was losing his battle with time.

"Hello, Sir," I said quietly.

He looked up at me with a half smile and said, "Hello, young man."

The determination that I had entered with started to dwindle as I sat down. He was so weak that I didn't want to upset him. Luckily, I didn't have to do much to get him talking.

He handed me the scrapbook and said, "It's time."

I took the book and flipped slowly though the pages. It was like he had expected me and knew that I had questions.

The photos were mostly black and white, and some had dates written on them. There were pictures of Mr. Rent when he was a young man, and I had been right. He was a good looking guy and built like a brick house. One of the photos had a young boy who looked a lot like someone I knew.

"That is Mr. Jim," he laughed.

I couldn't help but giggle at the skinny, freckle-faced kid wearing knickers.

"I should take that picture and show the entire staff," I joked.

Mr. Jim was such a jokester that I was sure that he could appreciate a poster size copy of that photo on the Niletree bulletin board.

As I continued to flip through the pages, I was surprised to find clippings about my father and his football career. I was even more surprised when I noticed an old photo dated 1947. It was Mr. Rent sitting on an old Ford and beside him was a very lovely young lady. I took the picture out of the book and looked closer at the image. My eyes began to tear a little. The young lady looked a lot like my grandmother, but that didn't make any sense. As I read the back of the picture it started to sink in. The words told the story: "C and C forever!" I thought back to my conversation with Mrs. Kessler and the fact that Mr. Rent had stayed in Rolling Hills for a few weeks during the great flood. I recalled that Mr. Rent had been in love with a widow and that the widow had kids. My grandfather had died in 1946 in a mining accident. The puzzle was coming together.

Mr. Rent didn't say a word. He simply sat and watched as the secrets were revealed. I continued to find new clues with every turn of the page. There were pictures of my father as a boy and as a teenager. There were even some photos of me as a baby. I finally broke the silence. "I don't understand, Sir!"

The old man took my hand and began his story.

"It was 1947, the year of the great flood. People were in danger and families were losing their homes. It had always been my job to cover such events," he said.

"I met your grandmother while helping to rebuild her barn. Your grandfather had died a year before and left her with fourteen children. Needless to say, she had her hands full," he added.

As he continued the story, my head was spinning with the new information. I certainly wasn't ready for what he said next.

"I fell in love with your grandmother and we saw each other for a few weeks. But I had a job in the city that I could not give up! Too many people depended on me, so I had to say goodbye to the one person that I loved the most." The old man wiped his eyes and grabbed a tissue.

"I didn't hear from her for a year, and what she told me changed my life! She had a baby, a little boy. The baby was mine, and I didn't know what to do. My life was complicated already, and I knew that she expected more of me, but I did all I could. I would send money every month to help her through the tough times, but I just couldn't be the father that she wanted me to be," he continued.

My elbow slipped off the chair, and I banged it on the side of the bed. I stood up and put my hand on his shoulder.

"What are you telling me, Sir?" I said hesitantly.

I already knew, but I had to hear it from him. The old man looked up at me with a tear in his eye and said, "Young man, you are my grandson!"

Now I was the pale one.

"You mean my dad was the baby, your baby?" I asked in disbelief.

The old man nodded and said, "I know it's hard to believe, but if you search your heart, you will know it's the truth!"

I took a step back and looked in Mr. Rent's eyes. My father had always told me that you could see what was in a man's heart by looking in his eyes. All I could see was love and sincerity.

"My father was born in 1948!" I exclaimed.

That fact had never crossed my mind. Grandpa had died in 1946. I guess it's just one of those things that you never think about until you have to. It had to be true. Dad was the youngest of fifteen kids and had obviously been raised to think that his father had died. Grandma had passed away ten years earlier and taken the secret to her grave.

"Please, don't tell your father. I would like to do that myself," he said.

"Oh my gosh, you are my grandfather!" I shrieked. I put my arms around him and hugged him hard as the news became a reality.

"I have some other things I would like to talk about, Sir, but I have to let this sink in for a while," I concluded.

The old fellow took a deep breath as if he had just taken a weight off of his chest. As I walked out, I felt happy and sad at the same time. I had found my grandfather, but I couldn't help but think about losing him. He was fading fast, and time was precious. I hadn't a clue just how precious it was.

Chapter Eighteen

As I lay there in bed, my mind raced. I tried to retire my thoughts for the night, but my brain was on overdrive. I kept thinking about my father and how he would react to Mr. Rent's secret. I dwelled on the facts that the old man had so bluntly revealed. Not only was this man my grandfather, he was some sort of mystical healer or something as well. I knew that in order to have some sense of sanity I would have to sit down with Dad and Mr. Rent for a long discussion. It was the only solution, and in my opinion, it was the right thing to do.

After a glass of warm milk and two sleeping pills, I dozed off only to be awaked by the disgusting ring of the telephone. As I ran to pick it up, my stomach wrenched. It was that familiar feeling of nausea that I would always experience with an early morning call. It was four o'clock, and that meant only one thing. Dad was sick again.

When I answered, I was not surprised to hear Lena's voice, but the message was unexpected.

"You need to get here as soon as possible," she said excitedly.

"There's a fire and we can't get to your father and some of the other patients!" she continued.

I hung up the phone in a panic. I dressed quickly and hurried to my truck. When I arrived there were firefighters everywhere. Niletree staff members had many of the patients huddled all together in order to keep them warm. I searched frantically for my father and Mr. Rent, but there was no sign of them anywhere.

"Lena, where's my Dad?" I cried.

"I'm so sorry! I don't know! I tried to get to his room, but the fire had spread too fast!" she apologized.

My heart fluttered as I heard one of the firemen tell his chief that the fire had taken the right wing of the complex. My father's room was on the right side of the building. I felt so helpless, and I began to weep.

"It's going to be okay, young man!" I heard his voice and turned to confirm the sweet recognition. It was Mr. Rent. He was sitting in a wheelchair with a white blanket over his shoulders. Beside him was his box of articles and the scrapbook. His face was blotted with black smoke as he tried to catch his breath.

I put my arms around him and cried, "Dad is gone! He's dead!"

I looked at Mr. Rent who was staring intently at the brick walls of the home, as if searching.

The old man took his hand and wiped my tears and said, "No! I see him! He will be alright! I promise you! He will be alright!"

As I knelt there beside his chair, I was overcome by his peaceful assurance.

"I wanted to be with you and your father. That is why I stayed here, young man," he said sadly.

Then, the old man stood. As I stared up at him, his frail body seemed to transform. His hunchback stance was altered as he removed the white quilt from his shoulders. He began to limp towards the entrance doors, and a firefighter yelled at him to stop.

"This is for you own good, old fella," the man said, as he attempted to restrain Mr. Rent.

The fireman's eyes widened as the old gentlemen lifted him off the ground by his shirt collar.

"And this is for your own good, sonny!" Mr. Rent replied.

As the fireman hit the ground, the old man's feeble limp graduated to a perfect sprint. Two police officers ran to catch him, but he jumped up. My heart pounded harder as the old man leapt several feet into the air to avoid his tacklers. He stopped at the entry doors and glanced back at me, then disappeared into the smoky darkness.

"The silly old fool. What was he thinking?" the fireman commented.

But I knew that Mr. Rent was anything but a fool, and I was beginning to understand just how special he was.

Minutes passed, and I feared the worst. Mrs. Kessler and Mr. Pyle held my hands as we prayed. I heard Lena yell to the director that everyone was out and accounted for except for my dad and grandfather. Then, it happened. The entire right side of the complex fell, as did my heart.

I turned to Mrs. Kessler and cried, "I've lost them both! I've lost my family!"

My worst nightmare had become a reality. My mind flashed back to the days when I had slept on my father's arm. I remembered our everyday conversations and the battles that we had faced together. He had been such a great father. And poor Mr. Rent; he hadn't had the chance to tell Dad the truth. It wasn't fair.

"Look," Lena exclaimed.

Every policeman, every firefighter, every person who witnessed the miraculous sight cheered as they appeared out of the fiery furnace. As the old man stumbled out of the building, I noticed that he was carrying something or someone. As his shirt was set aflame, Mr. Rent turned his head and blew out the remaining flames. His hair and body was still smoking from the intense heat. I wondered to myself how anyone could survive such an ordeal.

As he came to my side, he laid the body down on the cold grass. It was my father, and he was wrapped tightly in the old red blanket that was now blackened with soot. The words that the old man had written weeks before flashed in my head "The blanket will save your father!"

As a lump formed in my throat, I realized that the fire had not touched him. As Mr. Rent gasped for air, he collapsed beside of my Dad.

I shook my father who was unconscious, and yelled to the paramedics who were still helping the other patients. Nobody came to assist, so Mr. Pyle took over with his thunderous military voice.

"Attention! We need medics over here now!" the old man commanded.

Mr. Rent looked at me and smiled. "I told you he would be okay!"

He could barely speak, but he continued. "Use the crystal," he whispered and pointed to the box.

I ran and picked up the velvet bag and took it to the old man. He took the crystal out of the bag and held it above his head.

"You and your father," he coughed loudly. "Talk to Mr. Jim. He knows! He knows everything!"

The old man's eyes were getting heavy and his breathing more labored. He took my hand and lifted it to his heart.

"I love you, Grandson, and tell your Dad I loved him too," he gasped.

I noticed that the crystal's brilliant glow was fading, and only a glimmer remained.

"This is my life force given to me by my father! I now give it to my son," he chanted.

He waved the crystal, turned to Dad, and touched his forehead. As I watched the flickering glow dissipate, Mr. Rent closed his eyes forever. My old friend, my grandfather, was gone.

"Even heroes must die," I whispered.

My father's eyes opened, and he coughed. I kissed him and told him that he was safe now. I took the red blanket and held it to my chest and wept.

Chapter Nineteen

The hours that followed were very difficult. The nursing home had been saved and only the right wing had been blocked off. The residents were back in their rooms, and things were getting back to normal. The phenomenal occurrences that were so recent had already been forgotten by many. But I couldn't forget. Mr. Rent had died and with him he had taken many secrets. I missed the gentlemen in room 205.

I remembered what the old man had said about talking to Mr. Jim, and I looked forward to sitting down with him. Unfortunately, he had suffered some serious burns, and was still in the hospital. I would have to wait once again to find the answers.

I gazed down the hall to the old man's room and felt such sorrow. He had just wanted to be near his family in the end. It was such a depressing story that kept playing in my mind like an old tearjerker movie.

The right wing of the home was taped off even though my father's room and Mr. Rent's had not been destroyed. As I started to strip a piece of the tape off, I noticed Mrs. Kessler rummaging through the battered hallway. She was talking to herself as usual which always made me chuckle. She was standing near my Dad's room, so I walked up to her to assist in the inspection.

I was very pleased to see that all of my father's awards and belongings were untouched by the fire. I gave her a big hug in my celebration, and she giggled.

"Well, I wonder if Mr. Rent's room survived too," I said sadly.

"Mr. Who," the old lady snickered.

She looked at me with a baffled expression.

"Mr. Rent," I repeated.

She had no idea who I was talking about which led me to believe that the trauma of the fire had really affected her thinking.

She said, "Oh, you mean room 205!"

She hurried over to the door and mumbled something. I watched as she took the infamous marker out of her right pant pocket and began making the necessary corrections. As she walked away, she complained, "Those aides can't spell worth nothing!"

I stood there confused. Then, it hit me. I had never called Mr. Rent by his name. I had always called him Sir, and when I would speak of him to others, I would always refer to him as the gentleman in room 205. In fact, nobody had called him by his name during the entire few weeks that I knew him, not even Mr. Jim. Could it be that I had been mistaken for so long?

I walked slowly to the door, and inspected Mrs. Kessler's handiwork. I shook my head as I read the name and chuckled to myself in disbelief. I guess the old man had one last secret to reveal.

I had heard that Mr. Jim was feeling better, so I decided to go visit him in the hospital. As I entered the room, the camera flashed and once again the old comedian captured me with my eyes closed.

"How are you, Mr. Jim?" I asked.

He was a little beat up but in good spirits.

I told the old man what grandfather had said right before he passed.

Mr. Jim smiled and said, "Yes, I know the story. Do you have a little while?"

I poured two cups of coffee and stated, "I have all night."

Mr. Jim took a breath and began the story.

"Your grandfather and I worked together for forty years. He was the reporter; I was the camera. We covered a great many stories over that period of time, or at least I did. I would always get the picture, but he was always hard to keep track of, especially during the more exciting stories. I finally realized why my friend was never around. It seems that he had another job, one that took precedence over everything else. Your grandmother knew it. He couldn't even give it up for her," Mr. Jim continued.

The old man's eyes were wild as he told of how my grandfather had finally told him the secret.

"You don't work with someone for forty years and keep secrets," he laughed.

As I would snap the photos, your grandfather would get the story, but not before he made sure that everyone was safe.

The old man continued the story.

"When I had my stroke and couldn't talk, they put me in that nursing home. Everything that I had was taken from me in an instant. I would have rather died than spend my life in that place, so I turned to the only person I could count on, your grandfather. I sent him a letter explaining what had happened, and he was here the next day. He was a true friend indeed." Mr. Jim wiped his eyes and swallowed hard.

It was obvious that I was not the only one grieving.

"He helped me to get better. He used the crystal just like he did with your father. It was his life force, so in a way, he was giving up some of himself to heal me. It took its toll on him, so he was forced to stay at Niletree for a while to recuperate. Then, your Dad fell ill. When your grandfather found out that his only son was in the same hospital, there was no convincing him to leave. Even in his weakened state, he had decided to use whatever power he had left to cure your father. We both knew that it would eventually kill him, but he felt like it was his only chance to make things right," the old man paused to catch his breath.

"That is why every time he would visit your father, he would get weak," Mr. Jim said.

I thought back and Mr. Jim was right. At the time my father had made his vast improvements, the old gentleman had rapidly deteriorated. My grandpa had made the ultimate sacrifice. I couldn't help but smile though knowing the truth at long last. The man who had been a hero to so many and who had made the world a better place had died just the way that he would have wanted.

It was apparent that Mr. Jim was getting sleepy, and I had all the information that I needed. I told my friend to get better so that we could play some cards, and he smiled in agreement.

As I put on my coat, the doctor entered and said, "Okay, Mr. Jim, time for your medication!"

The old man pulled out a mini camera from under his quilt and caught the doctor unaware.

"Gotcha!" Mr. Jim exclaimed.

Chapter Twenty

"Hey, I have something for you two," Lena announced as Dad and I packed his things.

At long last, I was taking my father home. Lena handed me two envelopes. One was for Dad and the other was for me.

"He told me to give these to you two if anything ever happened to him," she added.

As I handed Dad the letter, I felt relieved. I hadn't told Dad anything about the gentleman in room 205. I guess I was just waiting for the right time. The old man had wanted to tell my father himself, and with the letter, he had the chance. I looked at Dad and prepared him for a shock, but I didn't give it away. I would allow the letter, his words, to tell the story that had been so long overdue.

I left my father alone to read while I retired to room 205 to pack up anything that I could keep as a reminder. I was pleased to see his box of newspaper clippings sitting in the corner. I picked one of the articles dated 1955 and sure enough the photo had been taken by Mr. Jim. The headline read, "Woman Crippled from Fall After Saving Baby!" As I studied the photo, I noticed a young lady lying on the ground with a familiar, old blanket wrapped around her legs. It occurred to me that my father was not the first to wear the healing quilt, the cape. I noticed that the scrapbook was still sitting on the nightstand as well. It was nice to have such personal items from him, and I knew that my father would appreciate them as well.

In the bottom of the box lay the crystal. I picked it up and held it close. I couldn't help but think back to the night of the fire and how the glow had faded away along with my grandfather. I put the precious gem in my pocket and carried the box to my truck. It was packed full of my father's belongings, and I barely had enough room for the extra items.

"Well, Dad, that's it!" I exclaimed.

I didn't comment about the letter, but his glassy eyes indicated what I had expected. There was plenty of time to talk about it later. I was just anxious to get out of that place, and I'm sure that Dad felt the same.

As we walked down the hallway, we stopped to say goodbye to Lena who was on her break. She came over to Dad and put her arms around him.

"Well, Iron Man! You did it," she laughed.

Dad hugged her and patted her on the usual spot.

"Better get your money's worth," she joked.

And, just like that, we were free. In a way, Niletree had been a prison. It was a place that we didn't want to be, but had to be. Now Dad was better and able to take care of himself. It was a true blessing to feel the breeze in our hair as we drove along. Even though our hearts were full with the possibilities of a new beginning, our thoughts were with the old man who had made it possible.

The funeral was on a Tuesday. News that the great man had fallen had spread all over the United States. He had evidently been an award-winning journalist along with his other lesser-known occupation. Still, you do not save that many people over that period of time and keep your identity perfectly concealed. But I guess he had touched just as many lives through his writings as he did by his heroic deeds.

There were flowers sent from all over the world, and people came from every corner of the globe. It was certainly an appropriate goodbye to the man who made so many sacrifices for the good of mankind.

Dad and I waited until the crowds were gone to pay our respects. Only Mr. Jim and some older lady that I didn't recognize remained in the parlor. She looked familiar, but I just couldn't place her, and I didn't really feel like talking to anyone. As Mr. Jim hugged her, I heard him tell her, "Keep in touch, Miss."

I came to find out later that she had been a reporter at the same newspaper office where my grandfather had worked back in the 1950's. She had been quiet the looker according to Mr. Jim.

Dad and I walked slowly down the aisle to say our goodbyes. He looked so peaceful laying there. It was one of those precious moments that can't be described with words. There were so many regrets. Grandpa had never gotten the chance to say "I love you" or "I'm proud of you." Those are the things that every son wants to hear from his father.

I reached into my pocket and gripped the crystal and placed it under Grandpa's hand.

"This belongs to you, Sir," I whispered.

Then, Dad handed me the old blanket that had been our source of protection for so long.

"We won't be needing this anymore, so let it protect you now, Grandpa," I added.

As I laid the red cape across his torso, the faded color seemed to transform to a brilliant crimson. I had seen him wearing it in a picture once, proudly upon his shoulders, flowing in the wind. Now it would cover him for all eternity.

We stood there for about an hour knowing that it was the last time that we would see him. We had never been good at saying goodbye, but now we were faced with the hardest goodbye of our lives. We had learned a very valuable lesson in the past weeks. Life is short and those that you love will not be with you forever. As I thought about all that had happened, I couldn't remember the last time that I had said it. My father was still alive. He had survived. Yes, even heroes die, but my hero was standing beside me. I turned and put my arms around him. "Dad, I love you! I just want you to know that!"

As I noticed the faint glow of the crystal, he patted me on the back and whispered in my ear, "I love you too, Son! I love you too!"

Epilogue

Life had returned to normal for the most part when I decided to go back to the nursing home to visit a few old friends. Mr. Pyle, of all people, had contacted me and wanted me to come see him about a very important matter concerning my grandfather.

It had been nearly two months since we had gone home. The memories of the place were still fresh in our minds, and even though it was difficult to go back, I longed to see the friendly faces that we had left behind.

I was curious as to what Mr. Pyle wanted to tell me, but of course, I had to visit Mrs. Kessler first. She was sitting in her rocker, talking to herself as usual.

I popped my head in and said, "Hi, Mrs. Kessler!"

She studied my face for a second and laughed. She walked over to me and gave me a big hug. It was good to see her smiling face again. We sat for a while and talked about all that had happened over the past few months. According to her, Grandpa was the talk of the nursing home. His heroics evidently had not been completely forgotten.

"We all knew he was special, but we had no idea that he was a real-life hero," the old lady laughed.

"I don't think many people knew that about him," I replied.

She went on to tell me that she had seen him once at the World's Fair back in the 1950's when she was a young lady.

"It was an amazing sight to see him soar! And his strength was remarkable!" she commented.

According to the old lady, a small girl had been trapped atop the Ferris Wheel, and she was dangling hundreds of feet above the ground. As the little girl fell, Grandfather took action.

"He came from out of nowhere, right out of the sky, and caught her just in the nick of time! Oh, what will the world do without him? He was one of a kind!" she said sadly.

I had often wondered the same thing. The world had relied on him for so long. Where would we turn when the next disaster hits? It was truly the end of an era.

I hugged the old lady and told her that I would try to come see her more often. I, more than anyone, knew that Niletree was a lonely place. Dad had survived it, but only because of the hero. Mrs. Kessler had nobody, and my life's lessons over the past weeks inspired me to do better, to give to others. Yes, the old lady deserved a friend and that is exactly what she would get from me from that point on.

"Always a pleasure, Mrs. Kessler!" I concluded.

I walked out of her room to find Lena and Max strolling down the hall towards the recreation area.

"Mad Max, how are you, buddy?" I inquired.

He ran to me and hugged me hard. Lena came to me as well and gave me the usual kiss. Max looked much happier than I had remembered him which made me smile.

"We are going to play bingo with Mr. Pyle," Max said excitedly.

"Well, I guess I'll just have to join you," I added.

We entered the room and Mr. Pyle sat in the corner with his board ready for action. Max ran and jumped up on the old man's lap.

"Hello, Mr. Pyle. It's been awhile." I stated.

We shook hands and looked into each other's eyes, both remembering that day. We would never forget it, but nothing had to be said.

He looked admiringly at Max and then back at me, as if to say thank you. I smiled and sat down beside him.

"So, you wanted to talk to me, Sir?" I asked.

"Yes I do, but not here. We will talk after the games," he replied.

Bingo lasted for about an hour, and when it was over Max had fallen asleep on the old man's chest. Lena picked him up and carried him over to a chair where he could continue to nap.

Mr. Pyle and I retreated to his room to talk. The old man closed the door behind him, so I knew that what he had to say was going to be a private matter.

"I know a secret, young man." he began.

Of course, I was anxious to hear it because I thought that all the secrets had been revealed. I leaned closer to hear him better.

He reached into the old cedar box and pulled out a red rag and put it beside him on the bed. Then, he reached under his pillow and exposed a small wooden box.

"Young man, will you push me outside to that old oak tree? I need a smoke," he said quietly.

I was on pins and needles, but I obliged the old fellow. He grabbed the objects and put them on his lap. He asked me to pick up his cigarettes from the nightstand and we were off.

The sky looked ominous with dark clouds painting the sky black as we made our way outside. There was a storm coming.

We sat there under the tree for a few minutes as he smoked and prepared. He seemed nervous which made me a little fidgety. When he took his last puff, he looked at me admiringly and said, "What do you think the world will do now without your grandfather?"

I told him that Mrs. Kessler and I had just had that conversation. The world had indeed been a better place, but there was nothing that could be done now.

The old man picked up the red rag and unfolded it. I was confused at first, but then I recognized it. It was my shirt, the one that had been used to stop Mr. Pyle's bleeding on that day.

"I don't understand, Sir! Why do you still have that?" I asked.

"It is the proof!" he replied.

I didn't understand what he was saying, but then he handed me the blood-soaked cloth.

"Look at it closely, young man." he said intently.

I did as he wished and examined every inch of it. My gut wrenched as I remembered that day and how close to death we had come. Then, I noticed it, a small hole which would have been directly over my heart. It was no bigger than a half of an inch, but it was a hole, a bullet hole.

"What are you saying, Mr. Pyle, that the bullet actually hit me?" I laughed.

The old man's face remained grim indicating that he was very serious. This made me very uncomfortable and I thought about leaving, but he interrupted my thoughts.

"That bullet didn't miss you that day! It bounced off of you! I saw your grandfather at the window when that madman shot you. He was just floating there and from his eyes, a red line of fire!" the old man stated.

It made sense that Grandpa was there. The gun had melted and I had suspected that he had intervened, but I had not been shot. I was sure of that.

"I believe you, Sir, about my grandfather. But that bullet missed me. I didn't feel anything. I didn't bleed. Do you understand that, Mr. Pyle?" I remarked.

Mr. Pyle continued to defend his position. He told me that it had been my grandfather who saved him that day back in the war. He had realized it after that day with the demon, after seeing him there at the window.

"I knew who your grandfather was after that day, seeing his eyes aglow! It was the same red flash that I had seen years ago on the day my brother was killed. Right before that tank blew up under me, I saw a flash of red that sheltered me from the bullets. Then, I was picked up and flown out of there. It was him. I am sure of it now," the old man muttered.

He stared at me, waiting for a response. It was very possible that all he was saying was true, but my mind rejected the obvious.

"Have you ever had a broken bone? Have you ever been hurt in any way?" the old man continued.

I thought back and could not remember a time which made me doubt my own beliefs. Mr. Pyle had a point. He went on to comment about my father and his lightning speed, his successful football career.

"That's why they couldn't bring him down, tackle him. Your father has it too, but only limited powers! Perhaps it skips a generation," he stated.

The old man opened the box, careful not to let me see the full contents. He pulled out a newspaper clipping that read "Player Suspended for Foul Play."

"I found this article on the internet when I was researching your father," he stated.

As he read it to me, I became even more confused. The article was about a college football player named Alex Luther who had been banned indefinitely from football. He was evidently the son of some well known millionaire from the west coast, so the story had been widely publicized. It told of how he had been the player who ended my father's career. With one fierce tackle, he had become famous as the man who killed the Iron Man.

Evidently, after that game was over, one of his own teammates betrayed him. The player told of how he had seen Luther stuff his gloves with some sort of greenish material. It turned out to be small, metallic green stones wrapped up in tape around each finger. It was hardly enough to injure another player, but college rules indicated that no foreign materials be placed on or in the uniform.

"You see! It was your grandfather's weakness, as it is yours and your father's! Every hero has enemies, and I guess one of them found out about your dad. Sometimes the best way to hurt a man is by hurting his family," Mr. Pyle exclaimed.

I had heard of the stone over the years, in the newspaper stories. I remembered all of the tales about how my father seemed to be superhuman on the field, all of the records he had set. It did make sense, but not me. I was a businessman and that was all that I would ever be.

"I am sorry, Sir. It may be true about my dad, but I am not my grandpa. I don't have any powers," I pleaded.

"What if you have them, but you just don't know or understand how to use them?" he questioned.

Once again, I entertained the notion and remembered. The day I hit the demon, I had felt like I almost flew into him. It had happened so fast that everything was fuzzy in my mind. Did I fly or did I run?

My thoughts reflected back to a spring day when Dad had thrown me a deep pass that I knew was not catchable, but I had leapt to try. On that day, I remember thinking that if only I could fly. I caught that ball, somehow I caught that ball. Did I fly?

I shook my head to get them out, those silly thoughts. No, I did not fly. I did not get shot. I had no powers.

Mr. Pyle looked at me and frowned. He put the clipping back into the box and folded up the bloody shirt. He had given up, and I was relieved.

"I guess there is no convincing you, young man. I guess the world is out of heroes. But there is one more thing I want to show you. I didn't want to, but you have left me no choice," he murmured.

My knees buckled as he pulled the gun out of the box. He pulled back the hammer and told me not to be afraid. I pleaded with him not to do it, but he continued to reassure me.

"This is a .38 and it will put a hole through just about anything, but not steel. It won't touch you, young man, I promise" he said with confidence.

I started to run, but I looked into the old man's eyes; they were honest. He was not crazy, but he was wrong about me; he had to be. I closed my eyes tightly as the old man took aim. Then, he fired.

I felt a sting, like a needle shot. I looked down at my shirt and took a breath. There was no blood, no pain, just a single hole where the bullet had pierced the cloth.

I looked at Mr. Pyle who was smiling from ear to ear. He lowered the gun and quickly hid it back in his box. Lena came running out to see where the shot had come from, but Mr. Pyle assured her that it had come from the woods behind us.

"Probably just a rabbit hunter. It's that time of year," he laughed.

I chuckled as well, relieved that I was still alive. Lena told us to try to dodge the bullet if it came our way. She laughed and went back into the home.

"Dodge a bullet, huh? You don't have to worry about such things now, young man!" the old man joked.

I stood there and tried to accept it. Mr. Pyle had been right. My life was simple, just the way I liked it. This would complicate things immensely, but I could not ignore it.

It would have to be done. I would have to figure it all out, the powers, how to use them. People needed help every day, they needed a hero.

"So, young man, what are you going to do now?" Mr. Pyle asked.

I looked to the sky, my heart beating like thunder. I had never tried, but had often dreamed about it. I turned my head to smile at the old man.

"I think I'll fly, Sir, right into that dark, dusty sky!"

Note from the Author

Life is short! That is an important statement to remember for all of us. I remember those days when I was a boy. Things were so simple then, passing the football in the yard and those infamous family vacations. As we get older, the world gets more complicated and sad. We lose those that we love, and go through many of life's surprises.

When my father fell ill in 2006, my world was shattered. He was my best friend, and I was forced to watch him die a little at a time. Watching someone you love suffer is one of the worst feelings in this world. It was a terrible time in my life, and it had a tremendous effect on me. As I held his hand during his last moments, I realized how fragile life is and how things always change.

I have always tried to treat people by the golden rule, but death is a wakeup call. Being polite is not enough. If you have ever been in a hospital or a nursing home, then you know the sadness that can dwell there. We all get old and one day, it will be us sitting in a lonely wheelchair. It is simply a fact of life.

We are so occupied by our jobs and ourselves that we rarely think about those who are going through these ordeals. Whether you are the child or the parent, it can be a very traumatic thing. There are those right now who are mourning the death of a loved one. There are others who may be visiting a sick relative and realizing that death is imminent.

After my father passed, I knew that my life would never be the same. He was no longer there to talk to about my problems. He simply went away, and I was not ready to let go. That is usually the case, I suppose.

My advice to you is to call your parents often and let them know you love them. Tell your family, and tell your friends. They may not be here tomorrow.

I would also like to take this time to urge you to get involved. Take time and visit your local hospital or nursing home to volunteer. Read to the elderly patients or sing with them. Remember, there are many of those patients who have nobody, and I am sure they would appreciate a friend.

I spent nine months in a nursing home with my father, and I met some wonderful people during that time. I was there every day, and I couldn't help but notice that some of the patients were very alone. They were waiting to die, just like Mr. Pyle in the story.

Often I would take my kids to visit my father, and I discovered a secret. Those old folks love children. I am sure it reminded them of their own children or grandchildren who had grown up long ago. I based the character, Max, on my son Trey who was always a big hit. And yes, he would run in the hallways and get into trouble from time to time.

It was so easy to make those patients smile. Whether it was a hug from Trey or a bag of peppermints, any attention was appreciated. It is funny how the little things we take for granted can mean so much to someone else. So, think about what you can do to help. Don't get too busy with life, and remember those who are less fortunate.

Life is short! Make yours special and help a few people along the way. Give to others, and you might just become the hero that you have always wanted to be.

Danny Harper
1948-2007

Danny Harper was born in 1948 in the small city of Spencer, West Virginia. He was one of 15 children raised in a two bedroom home on the outskirts of town.

With that many mouths to feed, times were often tough for the family. Other kids would make fun of Danny for his dirty jeans and his hand-me-down shoes. He spent most of his childhood defending himself against those who teased him and his family. Danny Harper was a fighter, no doubt about it.

As Danny entered his teen years, he made a decision. He would make something of himself. He would find a way to get noticed, to succeed.

His claim to fame came in the form of a football. He tried out for the Spencer High School team, and the rest is history. When the coaches saw him run for the first time, they knew that he was something special. He was a hungry player, ferocious. Even with his scrawny 150 pound frame, he was the kind of player every coach desires. He was all heart, and that is what it takes to be great in any aspect of life.

Perhaps it was because life had been so hard for the young man or because he had to fight on a daily basis, but Danny Harper made a name for himself. With every touchdown, with every crushing blow, he became known as "The Lone Spencer Halfback." The name was fashioned by a local newspaper writer who noticed that the skinny kid was so nimble that he could score without other players blocking for him. He was indeed a unique talent and everyone who observed knew it.

Going into his senior year, Danny was devastated by bad news. He was ineligible to play. Because his parents could not afford to have too many of their children in school at the same time, Danny had started a year late. He would be too old to play his last year of high school. His dreams of becoming All-State were shattered. He was heartbroken.

After High School, Danny played football for Glenville State College. He was once again doing what he did best, but it was short lived. With one blow to his knee, his athletic career was over.

Football came and went, as did his youth. He remained motivated throughout his life becoming a teacher, coach, and politician in his community. He had achieved success and his heart was at ease.

He was 58 when the stroke took him. For months, he fought a torturous battle, but it was one fight that he couldn't win. He died on a Sunday as I held his hand. It was a tender moment that I will never forget.

Danny has been gone for nearly three years now, but he is not forgotten. He lives on in our hearts and in the eyes of his grandchildren. I dedicate this book to him.

By the way, if you are ever in Spencer and drive by the Eventide Cemetery on Route 14, you will notice a tall oak tree that overlooks the valley where my father was born and raised. Beside that tree is the headstone of a great man and written on it are the words "The Lone Spencer Halfback."

About the Illustrator

Lewis A. White Jr. was born on August 25, 1973 in St. Joseph, Michigan. He attended high school in Summerville, South Carolina. He is a devoted husband and the father of three children: Jazzmen, Sierra, and Logan. He currently works as a rig hand, but is also an aspiring tattoo artist.

He is the son of a navy man and has lived in several different states. His experiences from traveling have greatly contributed to his art. Drawing has always been a passion and an outlet for the talented young artist. He currently resides in Spencer, West Virginia with his wife Melissa. Ironically, Lewis failed his Art class in high school.

Printed in the United States
151450LV00003B/2/P